UNTIL THE SUN GOES DOWN

Ike Hamill

UNTIL THE SUN GOES DOWN

Thanks to Christine for suggesting this book.

ISBN: 9781698972596

For Mr. King.
When I was a kid, your books scared the bejesus out of me.
I've been trying to recapture that feeling ever since.

PART ONE:

ALTRUISM

Flat Tire

(Here's what happened the other day.)

Here's what happened the other day:

The steering wheel jerked to the right when the tire blew. It felt like a tremendous animal, lurking in the tall grass that grew right alongside the road, had struck out and snagged the tire in its gnashing teeth.

The brakes locked up and a cloud of dust enveloped my rusty truck. The back end of the truck shifted to the left so I was effectively blocking the road. Granted, I had only been in the area a handful of days, but I hadn't seen another soul on that stretch of dirt road. I straightened the truck out anyway so I wouldn't be in anyone's way.

The rubber was grinding on the wheel—I could feel it.

I was sweating like a pig before I even opened the door. The only thing keeping me cool had been the moving air. Now that the truck was stopped, everything was perfectly still. If I had stood in one place for too long, I probably would have used up all the oxygen and suffocated.

The hood of the truck was about ten-thousand degrees. I made the mistake of touching it as I went around to see the shredded tire. I can't imagine how the thing just disintegrated like that. Strands of treacherous metal poked out from the rubber.

I glanced at my unblemished, soft palms, saying goodbye to smooth skin. There was no way I was going to change that tire without cutting and scraping the hell out of my fingers. Sweat rolled down my forehead and the middle of my back.

I'm a pretty self-reliant guy. Maybe that's the wrong word. It's not like I have a bunch of confidence in my own ability, I just hate interacting with strangers. There's that feeling when you have to extend yourself. You have to ask for help and admit that you are out of your element. I try to avoid that feeling at all costs. But in this case, with the sun practically burning the skin off the back of my neck and a shredded tire, I reached for my phone.

No signal.

I mean, *of course* there was no signal. I was maybe three or four miles away from the house, and there was no signal there. Even in the center of town there was only one bar on the display and I had crossed over a big hill before I turned off the Prescott Road.

I put my phone back in my pocket and dabbed my forehead with my shirt.

"Wait!"

There was something I had read before I moved to the middle of nowhere. It was about emergencies and cellphones. They said that if you dial 9-1-1, your phone will connect to whatever it can find, even if the tower is not on your network. They said that even if you don't have a SIM card, the phone will find a way.

Was this an emergency?

I sighed. No, this was not an emergency. People got in real trouble for bothering dispatch. Maybe if I was ninety years old, or had a small child or something. But I was, ostensibly, a perfectly healthy thirty-five-year-old dude, not obese or crippled. I put the phone away a second time.

There were three obvious choices—walk, change the tire, or try to drive on the rim. The third was the dumbest. I almost did it anyway just because it required the least amount of effort. That's how hot it was.

Rather, that's how hot it *felt*. I mean, there are plenty of hotter places in the world. One time I visited Arizona in the summer and it was like your lungs were cooking every time you took a breath. There were misters over sidewalks. Without them I'm sure that people would have collapsed and fried like an egg on the concrete. Still, people survived there and probably didn't drive on their rims when they got a flat.

The chrome door handle was almost too hot to touch. The hinges creaked and I felt around behind the seat, looking for the jack. I found the tire iron. The paint was chipped and rusted, just like the rest of the truck. I don't remember what year the vehicle was—seventy-two? When I registered it, the clerk laughed at the mileage.

"Get out much?" she asked.

The mileage I copied down from the odometer was exactly fifty-one more than the previous time the truck had been registered, and that was four years before.

"Oh. I don't know. I inherited it from my uncle," I said.

I'm not sure where Uncle Walt got the truck from. Like his weird old farmhouse—he had left me that too—it had just always been there at the end of the dirt road that didn't have a name, just a number.

Anyway, that's all I found behind the seat. No jack, just a rusty tire iron. The spare, I knew about. That was sitting in the bed of the truck. When I went to get the truck inspected, they had refused to put a sticker on it until I agreed to buy a spare tire from them. Afraid to be swindled, I had insisted on looking myself. The guy showed me where it would have been mounted if it existed.

"It was an optional accessory," he said, "but it would have been mounted up under here, between the axle and the bumper. Maybe your uncle ditched it when he put on this hitch."

I crouched down looking at the rusty bolts.

"Then how was it inspected four years ago?"

He shrugged. "You can go home and look for the spare if you want, but I have to fail the inspection. It's going to be another twelve bucks when you come back."

That's how they get you. If they find anything wrong, they have to fail the vehicle in order for you to drive away. Then, it's another fee when you bring back the truck to try to get it inspected again. Anyway, that's why I had a new spare tire in the bed of the truck. At the time, I had never expected to use it. Why would I? I can't remember the last time I had a flat.

It had never occurred to me to look for a jack. That had to be part of the inspection though, right? If they demanded a spare, why wouldn't they require a jack to be in the vehicle as well.

I sighed and then flinched back when I tried to lean against the hot metal.

Option two was out. I could walk or try to drive on the rim.

"Walk," I whispered.

(Like I said, it was hot.)

Like I said, it was hot.

Arguably, it wasn't *that* hot.

I grew up in South Carolina, in a fetid swamp vaguely near the coast. Now *that* was hot. It was different though. It was usual. You knew to take it easy certain times of day. You knew not to try to walk four miles of dirt road at one in the afternoon. You knew to stay in the shade and have some water around.

All of that wisdom flew out of my head at some point. By the time I moved to Maine to live in the house that I inherited from Uncle Walt, I was the kind of person dumb enough to be driving around in a fifty-year-old truck right into the teeth of a scorching hot day.

I had walked about fifty paces when I heard the crunch of gravel. Instead of turning around, I almost broke into a sprint. I was convinced that I would see the old truck rolling towards me, a limping predator out for my blood. Maine is that kind of place. It's the kind of place where trucks become possessed and hunt down newcomers on dirt roads in the middle of nowhere.

"Hey," someone yelled.

I turned and saw a bright, shiny new car sitting next to Uncle Walt's truck. The guy was waving at me.

My social anxiety had evaporated in the heat. I practically skipped towards the guy.

"Car trouble?"

"Flat. I don't have a jack," I said. I followed his eyes down and I realized that I was still holding the tire iron.

"I bet I can help with that," he said.

His car started to back up. The paranoid part of me spoke up and I knew that he was going to keep reversing until he got back to the Prescott Road, leaving me there. It would be within his rights. I probably looked like a crazy person, standing there with a tire iron and sweating through my shirt.

He didn't. The car swung in neatly behind the truck, his hazards popped on, and he got out.

"Wow, it's hot," he said.

His trunk popped open and he straightened back up. I tossed the tire iron towards the flat tire—no need to brandish it—and tried to lean against the fender again. It was still burning hot, of course. I rubbed my seared flesh.

He was rummaging in the trunk when he asked me something that I didn't quite hear.

"Pardon?" I asked, approaching slowly.

"It occurs to me that this little jack probably isn't going to do much to lift that truck. Here, hold this."

He handed me one of those little donut tires.

"I have a spare."

"It's not for your truck. I'm just hoping to add some height to this."

He held out one of those scissor jacks. For his small car, I'm sure it would be fine. With about fifteen inches of travel, the jack would easily get his car off the ground. For Uncle Walt's truck, fifteen inches wouldn't even unload the springs.

He had a handful of parts and the jack. I followed him towards the truck.

"Lay that on the ground."

He maneuvered the donut tire under the frame and then tried to balance his jack on top. After assembling the rest of the pieces into a crank, he began to extend the jack.

"Thanks for stopping. Maybe I could try your phone or something? I really don't think that this is going to…"

"No signal out here. That's why I stopped. If I had my car we would be all set. I have a really good…"

The tire tipped and the jack spilled to the ground.

"This is a rental," he said, gesturing to the shiny car. "Mine's in the shop. You're right, this isn't going to work. Can I give you a lift to town?"

"Actually, my house is just another few miles. If I could get there, I can call a tow truck or triple A or something."

I had said the wrong thing. His eyes stayed on mine while he reassessed me. Clearly, I was untrustworthy. If the roles were reversed, I'm pretty sure I wouldn't even have stopped.

"I'm supposed to be picking up my kid," he said. "I really don't want to be late."

"Of course."

"I'm headed to town anyway, so I don't mind dropping you off."

"Sure," I said. Politeness dictated that I ignore the obvious lie. If he was really in that much of a hurry, would he have stopped at all? Was driving another ten minutes really going to upset his plans? If the jack had worked, we would have taken at least that long to change the tire. No, when I suggested that he take me back to my lair, he had reassessed and decided that he wasn't going to let me lure him to a more remote location.

"Oh!" I said. "What if we use *my* spare to prop up the jack? It's taller and more sturdy."

He gathered up everything and stood.

"Then what would we put on the truck?"

"Oh."

It had to be the heat—I wasn't thinking clearly.

I followed him around the truck, towards his open trunk.

"So, yeah, I guess if you could drop me off in town, that would be great," I said. I was jabbering to fill the awkward silence of mistrust. "I can't imagine why there's no jack. I mean, don't they check that kind of thing when they inspect a vehicle? The thing, you know, just sat in my uncle's barn for..."

"It's not under the hood?"

"Sorry?"

"The jack?"

"Under the..."

"Yeah."

He tossed the stuff in his trunk, slammed the lid, and then veered around me. I went to the door of the truck, but he kept going. From the front, he popped the hood. It screeched and complained when he raised it.

"Here," he said.

I blinked at the dark cavity until I saw what he meant. The jack was mounted on top of the inside of the wheel well.

"Oh. I guess I never thought to look."

He reached in for it and I stopped him.

"I'll get it. It looks dirty as hell."

From that point forward, his job was mostly consulting and holding things. I was glad that he stuck around. If the jack hadn't worked or if one of the lug nuts had been impossible to turn, I would have still needed his help. Hell, without him, I wouldn't have known where to put the jack. It attached under the front bumper instead of back under the frame. I'm not usually dumb about such things, but the truck was older than I was.

Fortunately, the kind stranger—I still didn't know his name—seemed to know what to do.

"You're going to want to break the nuts first," he said.

"Of course."

I went to loosen them.

"Where you from?" I asked. I was thinking about the fact that he had a rental car. The heat had made me forget that he was only renting it because his own car was in the shop. He didn't have an accent that I could discern, but that wasn't surprising. A lot of the locals didn't have an accent.

"From here," he said. "The Depot."

I nodded and wiped sweat away with my shirt. The lug nuts were loosened so I went back to the front to start jacking.

"You'll want to put your parking brake on, if you haven't," he said. "These things will roll right away from the jack."

"Of course."

I went to do it.

"How about you?" he asked.

"Sorry?"

"Where are you from?"

"Oh. Originally, Mississippi, then South Carolina really. Virginia, Jersey, all over. I live here now. At the end of this road."

"Just you?"

Now, I was the one who was a little creeped out. There seemed to be some implication behind the question. If I was all alone, would I be able to defend myself in the middle of the night if someone should come creeping around? What if he was a serial killer, out searching for his next victim? One of those killers, BTK or maybe the Night Stalker, would find people with flat tires. Maybe I'm making that up.

"Just me," I said. I had intended to lie. The truth popped out anyway. "If you have to go pick up your kid, I think I have this."

"I have a minute. I'll just stick around until you get the new one in place."

"Thanks."

I wiped my forehead again. With the panic of being stranded wearing off, my social anxiety was coming back. I almost wanted to tell him to get lost, but that would have required a confrontation of sorts. I kept my mouth shut and kept working.

By the way, I was right about my hands. The metal sticking out from the steel-belted tires scraped up my palms when I tried to throw the ruined tire in the bed.

"You're bleeding."

I mean, of course I was. Blood dripped from my fingers. I got it all over the rubber of the brand new spare. The truck might not have been haunted when I started, but all that blood probably summoned a half-dozen demons into it by the time I was finished.

He handed me the lug nuts one at a time and I secured them before lowering the jack. Of course, he had to show me how to reverse the direction of the jack first.

"Thanks again," I said when the jack disengaged and clanked to the dirt.

I extended a hand to shake.

He cringed and put up his hands like it was a robbery.

"Oh," I said, looking down at the sticky blood on my palms. "Of course."

"Don't forget to tighten those nuts. You might want to check the torque when you get home."

"Uh huh. Thanks."

I waved and waited for him to walk away.

As soon as he turned around and drove off, my affection for him began to come back. He had saved me quite a bit of trouble, after all. The blown tire had metaphorically robbed me and left me sweaty and beaten. A priest and a Levite had passed me by and then this Samaritan stopped for me even though he had nothing to gain.

"I have to get out of the sun," I whispered to myself. "I'm going crazy out here."

House

(Nobody could possibly live here.)

Nobody could possibly live here.

I'm standing here looking at this dusty, peeling, relic of a house. All the windows are closed and the grass in the lawn is as high as the porch railing. But I can't stop thinking of the Good Samaritan—the guy who stopped to help me change my tire even though he was going to be late picking up his kid.

I wish I could remember the name of the man who used to live here.

Every time we passed, my uncle would say, "Wave hello to Mr. Such-and-such."

It was an old-sounding name. I can remember that much. There's no mailbox to help me out. Mr. Such-and-such and my uncle are the only two houses at the end of this long dirt road, so there's no mail delivery. Uncle Walt and Mr. Such-and-such had to go pick up their mail at the post office that's built into the back of the grocery store. Well, Uncle Walt doesn't have to anymore. I guess that's my job now.

I don't see any cars or trucks outside. Maybe on Monday I could go to the town hall and look up the property tax records or something. There has to be a simple way to find out if Mr. Such-

and-such is still alive and kicking.

"Or I could knock on the door," I whisper to myself.

Of course, that could lead to an actual conversation with a human. Wouldn't want to risk that.

This is all the Good Samaritan's fault. If that guy hand't stopped to help me change my tire, I wouldn't be out here looking at Mr. Such-and-such's house. I would be back at Uncle Walt's, separating junk from keepsakes.

The other day, I was listening to the radio. It was a station that calls itself, "The Mountain of Pure Rock." Apparently, "Rock" consists mostly of deposits of Molly Hatchet, sediments of Black Sabbath, and the occasional lode of Led Zeppelin. It's roughly the only radio station that I can receive during the day. During a "Solid Block" of George Thorogood, a public service announcement came on between songs. The announcer reminded me that, "Every heat-related illness and death is one-hundred percent preventable. Do your part. WTOS encourages you to check on people in your community today."

It is a really hot day. It isn't *South Carolina* hot, but for Maine, it's hot. And Mr. Such-and-such has all his windows closed. He has a pair of big trees flanking the house, but they're not doing anything to prevent the sun from streaming in his front windows.

I take a step through the tall grass. I'm sure legions of ticks are hitching a ride. I'll have to check myself carefully later.

Sweat is dripping down my back and rolling off my forehead again.

Six windows are looking at me: one from the attic, three on the second floor, and one on either side of the front door. My eyes keep going to the attic window. It's small compared to the others—just four panes over four panes. It has to be a thousand degrees up there, easy.

"I'll just knock, wait two-seconds, and then go home," I whisper to myself.

It's weird to talk oneself into something, you know? Who is speaking and who is listening? I guess it's my heart telling my head what to do.

My heart says, "Have some compassion. There could be an old guy in there, cooking from the heat. He used to be Uncle Walt's friend."

My head says, "If someone is in there, they've probably been dead for months, probably years. Do you really want to be the guy who finds the body? You just moved to town. Nobody knows you. Is this how you want to meet the local police?"

I actually don't have any idea if Uncle Walt was friends with Mr. Such-and-such. Aside from making us wave, Uncle Walt never talked about the guy. But they were the only two houses on this unnamed road. How could they not be friendly?

Sometimes if I take things in small steps, I can overcome my anxiety.

Step one—get to the door.

I walked through the most-likely-tick-infested grass and climbed the splintered steps.

In the shade of the porch, it was even hotter. It felt like the house itself had a fever.

Step two—knock.

(What qualifies as probable cause?)

What qualifies as probable cause?

Before I can get to step two, the knocking part, I notice that the door isn't latched. It's not technically *open* by any stretch. I can't see through a gap into the inside of the house. But there's too much space between the door and the frame, you know?

Back when I lived in New Jersey, I had this friend who would drop by all the time. Erin was my upstairs neighbor. I had a dog then. Or, maybe I should say that I lived with a dog. The dog came with the apartment and Erin came with the dog, so to speak. She had been friends with the previous tenant and she used to walk the dog for him. Anyway, Erin was sweet, but every time she let herself out of my apartment, she closed the door in the worst way. She would turn the handle as she pulled the door shut. When she let go of the handle, it was an absolute crapshoot if the latch would actually catch or not. So, sometimes I would come home and find my front door wide open.

Over the course of years, I found no way to train Erin to shut the door without turning the handle. She admitted that she was doing it. Even she had no explanation for the behavior. The closest we found to an explanation was that she, "Thought it was rude to slam the door shut." There's a huge gulf between pulling a door shut and letting the latch do its work and *slamming it shut*. It was weird.

I'm looking at this door, clearly not properly shut, and all I can think is that Erin must have visited. If there was even a breath of wind, it would blow the door open. Probably, I'm going to accidentally push it open when I knock.

To avoid that intrusion, I knock on the doorframe as loud as I can. The house looks like hell, but the doorframe is certainly solid. It absorbs my knock easily and barely conveys any sound into the house from what I can hear.

With a sigh and a deep breath, I prepare myself.

"Hello?"

The name comes back to me, echoing up from the back of my head.

"Mr. Engel?" I shout.

Wait, is that really his name, or some kind of weird joke that Uncle Walt was playing on me? Uncle Walt had a very dry sense of humor. Sometimes he would make up names for things and keep up the ruse for years and years. There's a sandwich shop in town and my uncle always called the place Hendershot's. Long after I learned how to read, I still thought the name of the place was Hendershot's. Then, one day I was looking at the sign and I finally took the time to realize that it was actually Henderson's. Even when I asked my uncle, he said, "No, no, it's Hendershot. They probably got a deal on that sign and just didn't care that it's wrong. Go inside and ask Mrs. Hendershot yourself.

I have no idea what the point of this joke was. I don't know if he was making fun of them or me. Uncle Walt wasn't a particularly mean person, so it's possible that he wasn't making fun of anyone. He just thought that it was a good joke to intentionally get a person's name wrong.

Now that the thought occurs to me, I'm pretty sure that the old man who lives here is *not* named Engel. It has to be an inexplicable Uncle Walt joke.

This time, I knock on the door.

As I suspected, the thing swings inward on the second knock.

"Hello? Are you home?"

I want to shout, "This is a WTOS wellness check on behalf of The Allman Brothers Band."

Instead, I settle for another, "Hello?"

The gap between the door and the frame is about an inch and a half. Angling my head, I can see the couch, a small bookcase, a coffee table, and a chair. There's a bar against the back wall. I don't see any sign of Mr. Engel.

"Hello?"

With my toe, I inch the door open a little more.

The heat coming out of that place is unbelievable. It's like opening the door of an oven. When I lean forward, I can feel the skin on my face tighten in response. I sniff at the air for signs of decaying flesh. It's silly, if you think about it. Mr. Engel probably went to visit relatives. Maybe he has a camp even farther north on the shore of some lake. Maybe he's visiting there.

But if any of those things are true, why is his front door open?

"Hello?"

(My imagination works overtime.)

My imagination works overtime.

I don't need it to work as hard as it does. I would like to be the kind of person who can walk away and not think about the house or Mr. Engel anymore. It's really none of my business. I stopped by, knocked, and even peeked inside. Isn't that enough?

I can picture him though. He closed all the windows and went upstairs to take a little nap in the hottest part of the day. Then, the house got hotter and hotter, he started to sweat, and before he knew it he was too weak to stagger back down and out of the house into fresh air.

I whisper, "But why is the door open?"

It can't be for ventilation. None of the windows are open.

There's no sign of Erin around—ha ha.

"Hello?"

Another idea: he opened the door to go out, a pain shot down his left arm, he staggered backwards and fell down behind the bar. If I lean to my right, I could probably see his shoes sticking out from behind the bar.

When I lean, I see nothing.

Mom used to always accuse me of having an overactive imagination. When we lived in Virginia, I told her about the man with too many garbage cans. He lived in the house behind us, across the alley. There were just way too many garbage cans across the back of his house. They were metal and they were spray painted with different numbers on the cans.

Mom said, "So what? He keeps a tidy lawn, I'm sure he's just a tidy person."

But those weren't the cans that he dragged out on Thursday nights for Friday pickup. The ones he dragged to the curb were greenish-black and made of plastic.

I think I was in fifth grade when I finally convinced my friend Matt that we should go check it out. He was supposed to stay at his father's house on Saturday nights, but he hated it there so he would often spend the night at my house. His father didn't mind. Not having Matt around meant that he could go out with his girlfriend. So, one fall night I said, "Let's wait until after Saturday Night Live and then we can sneak over there and look in those cans."

Matt didn't want to. He liked the idea of sneaking, but hated the idea of staying up past SNL. The sun always woke him up in the morning—he couldn't sleep if there was any real light in the room—so he preferred to fall asleep during the news. He would get mad at me if I laughed too hard. It wasn't a problem that year. Only five cast members returned to the show in 95, and none of them were funny. The new cast, like Ferrell and Meadows, would eventually become favorites, but it was a rough start that year. I waited up through the show anyway and then shook Matt awake.

"Seriously?" he slurred. "I *just* fell asleep and you're waking me up?"

He had been asleep for two hours, but I didn't bother to point that out.

"Come on, he turned out the light."

The porch light—a green bulb—had been turned off about midnight. Out there in the darkness, the cans were waiting to be examined. I put on my darkest pair of jeans and tossed Matt's clothes to him. Once he woke up, his mood improved quickly. Matt liked the idea of sneaking around in the dark. My mom was no issue. Back then, she used to crash hard most weekends on wine and pills. She said that the pills were for her monthlies, but she took them any time she didn't have to work in the morning.

"We'll go along the garage until we get to the bushes, then hug the fence to the alley. If we climb over the fence through the bush, we'll be behind..."

Matt walked right through the back door and started across the lawn. I eased the screen door shut so it wouldn't slam and then scampered after him.

"Hey," I whispered. "He's going to see you."

"We're still on your property," Matt said. "Who cares?"

I ducked behind the garage. Matt kept going across the

lawn until the got to the gate. Once he was in the alley, he took a right and it looked like he was going to head out towards the street. At the clump of bushes that I was planning to use for cover, Matt stopped.

We met there at the bushes and maneuvered ourselves until we could see through the branches to the windows of his house. The glass might as well have been spray painted black. We couldn't see anything through it.

"Wait, what is that?" I asked. It sounded almost like something tearing very slowly. I couldn't place where it was coming from until I backed up half a step.

"I'm peeing," Matt said.

"Well, stop it!" I said out loud.

The stream broke into staccato bursts as he wheezed out quiet laughter.

I could smell it. I really don't like the smell of urine—it has always bothered me. Before it could make me sick, I hunched over and darted to the next set of bushes. This wasn't the alley anymore. The place where I crouched was legitimately on the neighbor's property. I was trespassing.

Matt joined me a second later.

He made a series of gestures in the starlight and I understood. The bush covered us over to the picnic table and we crawled under that to get closer to the back porch. From there, we just had to dart across three yards of open space and we had our backs pressed against the side of the house. The trashcans were only six feet away.

Matt leaned close. "What's that smell?"

For a moment, I thought that the smell was still coming from him. It was ammonia. The night breeze brought it to my nose in full strength. It was definitely ammonia, but it was strong like smelling salts. I got my "bell rung" in a soccer game one time when I collided with one of my teammates. They used smelling salts to snap me back to reality. The odor was almost that strong.

"Cat litter," Matt said, answering his own question.

I didn't buy it.

I scooted down the wall. The smell got stronger and stronger until I could barely breathe. Matt was still a few feet away. He had his nose buried in his hands.

Applying steady pressure on the lip of the lid, I popped it off and the metal clanked. We held our breath as we waited for the sound of someone stirring inside the house.

My heart pounded in my chest, sure that the light would come on and we would have to sprint. I should have talked to Matt about an escape plan. If we ran towards the house, we would be caught for sure. The only smart thing to do would be to run for the alley and then take a left, working our way back around to the front of my house before we hid inside. That would give us an opportunity to lose any pursuit. It was too late to convey that plan to Matt now. I hoped he would think of it on his own.

But the lights didn't come on.

I had to summon enough courage to get up and look into the can.

We didn't even have a flashlight.

(We should have been heroes.)

We should have been heroes.

"Mom! Mom!" I said, shaking her. Her hair flopped around as her head rolled back and forth. I clicked on the lights and shouted again.

"Mom!"

I shook her so hard that her teeth banged against each other. Her eyes opened one at a time. The right one locked onto me and the left one wandered aimlessly across the ceiling.

"Whuh?"

She squinted and blinked hard and then tried to push up to her elbow. On the third try, she got it.

"Mom, we went across the alley because we saw a raccoon trying to get into those trashcans and we wanted to scare it away."

This was the best story we could come up with. The truth would have been easier.

"The raccoon opened up the lid and we found body parts in there, Mom. I told you that the guy was up to no good. He must be killing people and maybe eating them or something. Who knows how many people he has stuffed into..."

She cut me off by turning off the light.

"Go to bed," she said into her pillow.

If I ever forget what it was like to be a kid, this memory brings it right back. Kids have exactly zero power and zero credibility. The most momentous, life-changing event can happen to a kid and a parent will just tell them to shut up or maybe try to mollify them with some platitude. What we found was legitimately the most horrifying thing either of us had ever seen in our lives. I don't know what kind of life Matt has led recently, but I would be willing to bet that he still thinks about what we found. I know I still do. And I still remember exactly how frustrated and helpless I felt when my mother wouldn't even listen to me that night.

I turned on the light again.

With her eyes still shut, she reached to turn it off.

Matt pushed the plastic bag into my shoulder. I took it and shoved it into the path of her hand. Before, I hadn't even wanted to touch the bag. What was inside, mashed against the clear plastic, was too horrific to contemplate. My mom's hand hit the bag and she gave the thing a squeeze.

Behind me, Matt gagged.

Mom opened her eyes and jerked back.

I imagine that she cursed something, but her words were unintelligible. She jerked back, pushing her blankets and pillows into a tangled jumble as she retreated across the bed. I looked down at what I was holding and I dropped it. The seal on the bag split and the odor began to fill the room immediately.

Matt gagged harder.

"What?" she screamed. "What is it?"

Despite the smell, I forced myself to bend over to try to shut the bag before the disgusting fluids ran out onto the carpet.

Matt's voice croaked as he gagged again, but he managed to say, "We think it's a foot."

There was absolutely no doubt that it was a foot. One might debate the age and the sex of the previous owner, but to doubt the nature of the body part was silly. We had found a severed foot, marinated in blood and brown goo, in a plastic bag. Matt had said "we think" because that was easier than being definitive. To admit that we knew for sure what it was, we had to admit the terrible circumstances that must have led to it being in a plastic bag.

"Get *rid* of it," my mom yelled.

"Mom, we have to call the police."

"GETRIDOFIT!" she screamed in one ragged burst of sound.

I sealed the top again. We used the same kind of bags sometimes when we picked strawberries and my mom wanted to freeze a bunch. The smell was already in the air though. Sealing the bag didn't magically make it go away.

"Get. It. OUTOFHERE!"

I backed up with the bag pinched between my fingers. I almost dropped the thing again, but recovered and took it to the bathroom where I gently lowered it into the sink. The bone protruding from the skin and muscle didn't look like it had been broken. It looked cut.

My mom's adrenaline must have overpowered the wine and pills. She pounded into the hall while wrapping herself in her robe.

"Explain that thing," she said. Her accusing finger pointed at me, not the bag.

"We found it in one of those cans behind the neighbor's house. Remember how I said that he wasn't using those cans for trash? How he uses plastic ones for the trash? We looked in the metal ones, and this was there. He has eight cans now. There's probably more in them."

"Why would you... What is it doing *here*? In my *house?*"

"Because we have to call the cops. They need evidence," I said.

This time, she didn't yell. She didn't point or scream. Her voice sounded low and calm. With my mom, that's when you really had to worry. Her deepest anger didn't glow red, it turned absolutely black, absorbing heat and light like a black hole.

"Go to your room."

(Life is unfair.)

Life is unfair.

Our monumental discovery was treated like a terrible, shameful secret.

My mother plowed us into my room and shut the door. A minute later, she pulled us out and took us into the kitchen. The bathroom door was shut. Some of the smell had leaked into the hall. She put my hands under scalding water and scrubbed my fingers for me until I was squirming and pulling, trying to get away. To my mortification, she did the same thing to poor Matt. He didn't complain, but his face was wrinkled up like he could still smell the awful bag.

Then, with our hands washed and dried, we were banished to my room again.

Even with my head stuck out the window, I couldn't see the front of the house. Matt saw the headlights sweep across the garage door.

"Somebody is here," he said. He pressed his ear against the door and I did too. My mother's voice came in rapid bursts. The police were calm and condescending. I could imagine the smug look on her face when she opened the bathroom door. After that, the police didn't sound so calm.

Waiting was pure torture.

I wanted to open the door so badly.

"He's going to know it was us," I whispered to Matt.

Matt shook his head.

"Yeah. He's gonna. When the cops go over there and look in the cans, who is he going to think turned him in?"

"So what?" Matt asked. "He'll be in jail."

"That's not how it works though. Innocent until proven guilty, you know? They have to have a trial and that takes months or years. Until then, he's going to be after us. He'll get revenge on us for ratting him out."

"You watch too much TV," Matt said. I could tell he was nervous too. Then I really started to get scared. Usually, I was the alarmist and he was the one to tell me to settle down. When *he* was nervous, bad stuff was coming.

The door opened and we both screamed.

The officer pointed to Matt and then curled his finger, telling Matt to go along. I had to go to the bathroom really bad at that point, but what was I going to do? The bathroom was probably roped off as a crime scene. Besides, I hadn't been granted permission to leave. I figured it all out in a flash—the cops were going to separate us, get us to turn on each other, and then pin a crime on one of us. The first one to confess would probably get off light.

I couldn't stand it anymore. I opened my window and let the fall wind roll in. It was the only way I could stop the feeling that I was about to suffocate. If they had made me wait another couple of minutes, I might have run for it. I pictured it as I stood there, drinking in the chilly air. I pictured slipping through the window, dropping to the ground, and sneaking between the police cars that were stacked in the driveway. I could be off and hitchhiking before they even raided the neighbor's house. I would be like the Incredible Hulk, wandering from place to place, always in fear that someone would learn my secret.

I was about to try it when the door opened.

Matt came in, head down and shuffling. They called me

three times before I eased my grip on the windowsill and went with them.

The questioning felt like it took hours. In retrospect, they were being incredibly kind and gentle, asking what happened without accusing me of trespassing. It didn't help. I was so paranoid that they were trying to lure me into a trap that I answered everything with clipped, one-work answers. They got angry and left me alone.

Two officers stayed with us down in the TV room in the basement while the others rolled out.

They did a great job at terrifying us. If we told anyone what happened, it would weaken the case against the guy. That's what they warned us. A single word about what we had found might put the guy back on the street. Nobody finished the thought—that if he was set free, he would immediately hunt after us for revenge. Matt and I had already pieced that fact together, so we swore our secrecy to the police and later to each other.

Neither of us said a word. Matt didn't even tell his parents.

Months later, the story came out on the news and everyone claimed to know about it. The girl who lived across the street from the murderer was a couple of grades beneath us. She said that she watched out her window while the cops shot their guns through the walls and killed everyone inside. Her story lost credibility when kids looked at the house and saw that it didn't have a single bullet hole in the siding.

Another kid said that his uncle was one of the victims in a trashcan. When he couldn't come up with the uncle's name, his story was debunked. By the time that Matt and I thought to tell our side of it, nobody believed us. Our story was one of many implausible tales that was circulating.

Our shameful secret faded away. Our contribution to the safety of society was never recognized.

I suppose it was for the best. Rumor has it that the man wasn't acting alone. He was working for organized crime or something. Mobsters supposedly ordered a killing, my neighbor fulfilled the order, and the mobsters would eventually come to remove the trashcans. Maybe it was just another tall tale. Just in case it wasn't, it's a good thing that nobody knew about the two boys who cracked the case.

(What is that noise?)

What is that noise?

"Is anyone home?" I shout. I swear I heard a noise—a groan or something—from inside the house just as my shout is fading out. What are my options? I want to go home and forget about all this. I can't do that. I suppose I could go home and call the police. That's a really unappealing idea. First, I would have to track down the non-emergency number, right? You can't just call 9-1-1 because somebody left their door open on a hot day, right?

Also, there's a voice that lives down in the darkest part of my heart, and that voice whispers, "You won't get credit." That sinister voice is still upset that I never got credit for being right about the neighbor across the alley. Matt and I had discovered a murderer and nothing good ever came of it. I mean, aside from taking a monster off the streets, nothing good ever came of it.

I reach out and pause just before my fingers touch the door. It would be rude—maybe even illegal—for me to push my way into a stranger's house. Maybe if the door were wide open, there would be no harm in my wandering inside to check on...

As I ponder the legality of walking through an open door, I reach out with my toe and swing the front door the rest of the way open. Now I can see everything inside.

There's a sign on the wall over the bar.

"Work is the curse of the drinking class."

Through the doorway to the left of that, I can see a counter and an oven that has to be decades older than I am. Stairs run almost up the center of the house. Leaning in, I can see what might be a dining room on the left. This place is nothing like my uncle's house. The floor plan of this house seems completely intentional. Uncle Walt's house, in comparison, accreted around some tiny nugget of a dwelling that was planted two-hundred years ago. In his kitchen, the pine floorboards still wrap around the original hearth that's no longer there. I suppose I should stop thinking of it as "Uncle Walt's House." It's mine now.

"Mr. Engel?"

Is it the echo of my voice, or was that another moan?

Entry

(Something changes when I cross over.)

Something changes when I cross over.

I shift from concerned neighbor to busybody. One might even call me an intruder.

Usually when I enter a house I take off my shoes. It's not something I ask my guests to do, but I almost always do it when I'm visiting. I don't even consider doing that now. It seems inappropriately intimate to walk around Mr. Engel's house in my socks without him there to grant permission. Besides, I might have to leave in a hurry.

"I'm coming in. I want to make sure you're okay."

Hot, humid, and suffocating. The air inside the house barely seems breathable.

There's a glass on the bar with a tiny ring of brown in the bottom. Whatever was in there has evaporated. Next to it, the TV Guide doesn't have any dust on it that I can see, but David Schwimmer and Jennifer Aniston are on the cover. The magazine has to be at least twenty years old. I lean forward to see if Mr. Engel has collapsed behind the bar. Somehow I can picture it—the old man has a heart attack while he mixes a drink and gets ready for an evening of watching Friends. If that's when

Until the Sun Goes Down

he went, the body will just be a skeleton in overalls.

Nothing.

I let out a relieved sigh.

My hand is resting on the bar. I use the bottom of my t-shirt to wipe off the prints, exchanging fingerprints for DNA, I'm sure.

"There's no dust," I whisper. "He has to be alive."

With one more step, I'm crossing the threshold to the kitchen.

"Mr. Eng..."

I don't finish the name. He's on the floor in front of the sink.

                    (I rush to him.)

I rush to him.

My knees slam down to the vinyl floor and I reach for his hand. The man is so wrinkled and dried up that I'm afraid I'm too late. Maybe this is just a desiccated corpse, turning into human jerky in the heat of the kitchen. He's on his side and facing towards the cabinets. I can't see his eyes. A tiny moan escapes him when I touch his hand and he starts to roll towards me.

"Mr. Engel, are you okay?"

What a stupid question to ask.

What's he supposed to say? "Why, yes, good sir, I'm just taking a quiet nap on the sticky-hot vinyl of my kitchen floor. I often lounge here in the summer. Please forgive my sleep moans."

I help him roll to his back and his eyes scan the ceiling. The one closest to me is milky white. The other is yellow and brown. His good eye locks on me for a second and then slides off again. His lips smacks and he works his tongue around like he's trying to form words.

"Mr. Engel, you hold on, okay? I'm going to call for help."

I pull out my phone. Even though I don't get any signal here, I still slipped it into my pocket when I got out of Uncle Walt's truck. No bars are showing on the display. It's time to test out the idea that 9-1-1 will always work.

It doesn't.

My phone complains of no signal. There's a message I've never seen before, informing me about emergencies. I don't bother with it.

"Where's your phone, Mr. Engel?"

All I can think about is the phone in my Uncle Walt's house. I know precisely where that is. If I jump back in the truck and drive about five minutes, I could call from there.

He looks like he might not last that long.

I see it. The phone is mounted on the wall right next to a door that must be a closet or pantry or something. It's one of those old, heavy, rotary phones with a long and curly cord. I lay his hand down gently and spring to my feet. When I dial the nine, it feels like it takes an entire minute for the huge dial to rotate back around. My adrenaline is pumping so hard that everything is moving slowly.

The line clicks and buzzes and then an angel answers.

"9-1-1 what's your emergency?"

"My neighbor has collapsed on his floor. I think he has heatstroke or something. Maybe a heart attack. I don't know."

"What's your address?"

I give her the road number. I don't have any idea what the address is. "Tell them it's the white house on the right before the end of the road. It's the only other house on the road except for my uncle's. Mr Engel—that's his name. I don't know. Can you look it up or something?"

"Absolutely," she says.

She could have said a lot of things. "Stay calm," would have been appropriate. I love her for choosing that word instead.

"Now, how is Mr. Engel? Is he breathing? Can you feel a pulse?"

I don't want to return to him. I've handed off this problem to the angel on the phone. It's unfair that I have to go back to him and again violate his personal space as well as my own. I have to do what the angel says though.

I lower myself to my knees, barely tugging the phone cord. This is the kind of cord that could reach all the way to the front porch if required. The angel waits while I lean close to listen for his respiration. She says, "Good, good," when I count off Mr. Engel's pulse.

"Do you have water handy? Can you wet a towel and begin to cool him off."

"I will. Someone is coming, right?"

"Yes. Help is on the way."

I tuck the phone between my ear and my shoulder and grab the dishtowel that's hanging next to the sink. There are two big knobs—one for hot and one for cold. The tap squeaks as I rotate it and the water sputters from the spout between blasts of air. Below me I can hear the pipes chatter and groan. The sound is matched by Mr. Engel.

"Sir?" the angel asks.

"It's the pipes. The pipes are making that noise."

"Are you still there sir?"

"Yes. I'm waiting for the water to cool a little before I wet the towel."

The intermittent stream from the spout is warm. It almost feels oily or something. It's too slick between my fingers.

"Sir? Are you there? I'm going to stay on the line. Are you..."

The phone clicks several times and then the buzzing dial tone comes back.

With another blast of air, I finally get some cool water from the tap. I soak the towel until it's dripping and then shut the water off. The receiver is still buzzing in my ear as I kneel next to Mr. Engel again.

"Here," I say, lightly dabbing the wet towel on his forehead.

It was better when the angel was in my ear. It was like she

was possessing me—working through me. Now, it's just me and Mr. Engel again. I can't disconnect from the reality of the suffering man in front of me.

His dry lips are cracked and split. In the bottom of deep chasms I see dark red that must be muscle tissue. The hand I'm holding resembles tissue paper draped over bird bones. Mr. Engel could blow away in a stiff breeze.

The phone is still buzzing for a moment and then it clicks again. I set down the receiver and the cord recoils it back towards the wall. It's retreating before another strike.

When I dab his face and forehead, he blinks and swallows.

"You're thirsty," I say, a little too loud. "Hold on."

I push to my feet, thinking of Kimberly. Until now, I have been desperately trying to *not* think of her. They only let me give her ice chips. From the panting and rhythmic breathing, her lips had been dry too. They were nothing compared to Mr. Engel's lips, of course, but Kimberly had asked me to put ice chips against her lips while she battled the contractions.

Mr. Engel's refrigerator is shaped like a giant tombstone. There is no freezer door, from what I can see. When I open the fridge, the handle rotating on a hinge to release the latch, I see that the freezer door is inside the compartment. Inside it, I find a metal tray with cubes. I free a couple and return to Mr. Engel.

He swallows reflexively when the cold hits his lips. He squinches his face—maybe the ice stings him. Then his tongue chases the cube when I pull it away. I lay it across his lips again.

Behind me, the phone begins to squawk.

Mr. Engel's eye follows me as I jump up and return it to the cradle.

I dial again.

It rings and rings and doesn't connect. I hang up and try again.

"I can't get them to answer," I tell Mr. Engel. When I look down, I'm startled to see that he has turned his head so he can watch me at the phone. I put the phone back and return to his side. With the towel in one hand and ice in the other, I dab and soothe.

"They said they're on their way," I said.

He blinks.

His eye assesses me.

"I'm your neighbor," I say, in case that's what he's wondering. "Walt's nephew? My uncle left me his house."

He makes a sound through his parted lips.

"Sorry to barge in on you," I say. "I came by to make sure you were okay in the heat and your door was open. I thought I heard you calling for help."

He makes a low moan and I nod.

I pull the ice away.

"Are you... Are you trying to say something?"

His teeth come together and he makes a tiny hissing sound. "Ice?" I ask.

It's a good guess. He nods a fraction of a fraction of an inch.

I put the ice back to his lips.

(He was on the floor.)

He was on the floor.

I have to assume that he fell. Given that, I have to assume that he might be injured. Given *that*, I'm not sure I should move him. I want to take him outside, where there might be a chance of air moving around. I'm sweating so much that my own lips are beginning to feel dry. It almost hurts to blink.

Mr. Engel isn't sweating at all. When I lean over to listen to his breathing again, he almost smells like a towel, fresh from the dryer. If all old people smelled like that, people would probably take better care of them. When Kimberly was in her second trimester, her friend Bethany gave birth. I practically had to drag Kimberly away from that child. All she wanted to do was smell that baby's head.

I wonder why nature didn't engineer a similar smell for

dying people. It's probably because wasting effort on old people isn't an advantage for the species. I understand why nature is heartless, I suppose, but it seems especially cruel that it gave us empathy so that we can understand the depths of the heartlessness.

"I don't know how long it will take for them to get here," I tell him. His eye seems to widen a tiny bit. I hastily revise. "But I'm certain it will be any second. All you have to do is hold on for a few more seconds and they're going to take good care of you."

When I stop talking, I can hear him breathing.

There's a tiny pause after each exhale before he starts pulling in air again. I don't like it. My heart stops each time and it feels like the gap is growing.

"You need to stay with me, Mr. Engel," I say.

I don't tell him what I'm thinking about. In the delivery room, everyone tried to make me think that I had an important role in the process.

They would say things like, "Come on, Dad, you have to help her breathe."

Like that's a thing.

Then, with no notice at all, the demeanor of the doctors and nurses changed. They all saw something that Kimberly and I were completely unaware of. She was breathing and pushing, just like she was supposed to, and then chaos took over. Suddenly, I was pushed out of the way and the medical professionals descended. More masked people appeared. Kimberly faded as she descended into herself. The pain and effort disappeared from her face and the doctors fought hard to drag her back to the surface.

"When I was a kid," I say, "I used to come up here a couple of times a year. My uncle bought his house right out of college, so it seemed like he had been there forever. Every corner of his house is distinctly him, you know? I think you were already living here when he moved in, right?"

He blinks and I take that as a yes.

"It was a magical place for me—nothing like the suburbs at

all. The first time I came up here alone, to stay with my uncle for the whole summer, I was thrilled during the day and terrified at night."

I smile at the memory.

"The sound that the train makes when it's going across Bartlett Road. The way they always blow the whistle before they round the corner? It's such a haunting sound."

Mr. Engel's lips part to a smile.

"I would always imagine that they blew the whistle to clear the vampires off the tracks, you know?"

I've never admitted this to anyone. It's such an absurd, little kid thing to think.

He is still smiling and he nods again. Maybe he's just reacting to the pleasure of the ice on his lips. A little moisture is rolling down from the ice cube, into his mouth. When Kimberly went into surgery, they told me that it was a good thing that she hadn't had anything to eat or drink because it would mean that putting her under anesthesia would be less dangerous. They said it like it was some personal decision that I had made.

"Someone told me that vampires lurked in the woods up here. It was a friend of mine down south. I know that he was just messing with me, but a part of my brain kept telling me that rumors usually germinate from a seed of truth. I've never been to Romania. I've never been in any part of Eastern Europe. But I always imagined that Maine is the closest thing we have to that kind of terrain. I'm probably wrong. Anyway, I would always picture a swarm of mindless vampires that had descended on a big moose as it crossed the tracks. The train engineer couldn't tell exactly what was going on, but he could see the people on the tracks. He would blow his whistle, warning them away and he would try to slam on his brakes. Why am I telling you this?"

I know why, though. I'm filling the silence with this story because it means that I won't have to listen to his breathing. Also, his good eye is focused right on me. I don't know if he even knows what I'm saying, but the story is keeping him present. I just need him to stay conscious until help arrives.

"After the first night, I should have realized that there was no way that my story could be true. There would have been something in the paper about how the train was stopped, right? The vampires would have swarmed the train and drained the guy's blood."

Mr. Engel's eyebrows twitched.

"I know, it's a silly story. I was a kid. That first week that I spent alone with my uncle, I was so scared every night that I probably only slept three hours total. I would nap in the truck when we went to the lake. I curled up in the bow of the boat with all the life preservers and spiders. We went fishing and hiking. What a great time."

I sighed.

"Uncle Walt didn't have a job. He didn't seem to have much money either but it didn't bother him any. I always got the impression that he was just living alongside the rest of society, you know? He had opted out of jobs, taxes, income, budgets, and all that. He had his garden and he didn't buy much. He never took vacations or anything—why would he? As he always said, 'My favorite place is here.' It would have been silly for him to leave that behind. He was wrong about that though. Because he never left, except to go to the store or the lake or whatever, he never knew the profound excitement and anticipation of returning. When we would turn off Prescott and onto this road, my heart would soar and I would feel it all the way down to my groin. Pure contentment was ahead and the only way to really appreciate it was to leave and then experience the joy of coming back. I'm almost sad for him that he never got to have that feeling."

I am sitting on my right leg with my left leg out to the side. With one hand I'm caressing Mr. Engel's lips with the ice cube. He lifts his hand and finds my free hand, giving it a squeeze.

"Are you feeling a little better?" I ask.

He nods. It's a good, energetic nod this time. His tongue sweeps over his lips, pulling in some of the moisture from the ice cube and he gears up his mouth while his Adam's apple bobs.

I lean in closer, convinced that he is going to say something.

I'm right.

His breath wheezes at first while he tries to get his vocal cords going.

"Yes?" I ask.

His voice is so quiet that it's almost subsumed by the hum from the refrigerator.

"The vampires," he manages to say.

There's such a long pause that I'm convinced that he's finished.

"The ones I used to imagine at night when I was a kid?"

He nods and I figure that he wants to hear more about that story. I open my mouth and I'm silent for a moment, trying to think of what more I can say. Like I said, I never told anyone about it. The fear was just a misplaced manifestation of separation anxiety, I'm sure. I never felt all that close to my mother, but until that point in my life I had never really been apart from her. She was my only parent so of course I was attached to her. Until I was ten, I would sometimes wake up in her bed, completely unaware of whatever nightmare had driven me to seek that comfort. So when she sent me away to stay with my uncle for the summer, I had invented something to be afraid of at night. I latched onto the stupid story that Matt had told me and my imagination ran wild.

I'm about to tell him a version of that when he speaks again.

"They're in the cellar," he whispers.

PART TWO:

DENIAL

Vampires

(It takes me a second.)

It takes me a second.

I have to admit, for a moment it feels like the temperature of the room has dropped about fifteen degrees. My sweaty shirt feels cold against my skin. My fingers and toes are almost numb. I take a deep breath and force myself to hold it for a second.

Some people are blessed with strong parents and they get to learn from that example. I was blessed with a mother who was meek and victimized because of it. I didn't see it that way when I was a little kid. I didn't see how she was complicit in letting the world roll over her. In my mind, she was never at fault. There were mean people everywhere. They should have left my poor mother alone.

By the time I was in school, when I learned that one had to stand up for oneself, my perspective changed. Suddenly, I saw that my mom was inviting people to take advantage of her because she would never stand up for herself.

Then, a really weird thing happened. My mother began to evolve. She stopped drinking so much and stopped taking pills. Instead of medicating herself enough so she could hide in bed, she actually began to speak her mind and say no when people tried to pull a fast one. I stopped hating her and began to cheer her on.

She said something really interesting to me one day.

"Everyone is full of crap until proven otherwise."

That was a step beyond how I saw the world. Her cynicism had progressed so far that it had blossomed into arrogance. I adopted her new slogan immediately.

Along the way, I must have forgotten.

This man on the floor, who is clearly delirious and hallucinating, has just told me that there are vampires in the cellar. For a terrible, shameful moment, I let that idea frighten me. Blame the little kid who came up to Uncle Walt's every summer. That little kid still occasionally whispers in my ear.

"It's okay, Mr. Engel, the sun is out," I say.

His wide eyes blink and he relaxes his grip on my hand.

"I turned off…" he says. I follow his eyes to the far side of the room. There's a fan there. Its metal blades aren't turning. "The fan. They don't like heat."

"*They* don't?" I ask.

"Vampires," he whispers.

This is potentially really bad news for Mr. Engel. If he turned off the fan *before* he collapsed from heat stroke, then his psychosis must predate this illness. That could spell bad news for his future. I imagine myself going through his things, looking for an address book of a daughter or cousin. They might have to get him declared unfit so they can put him in assisted living or something.

I'm being silly though. He only latched onto the idea of vampires because I mentioned them. That can't be the reason that he turned off the fan. I release my hand from his. The fan isn't turned off, it's just unplugged. The cord is two cloth-covered twisted wires that end in a rubber plug. I pinch the thing between my fingers, hoping that it doesn't electrocute me when I try to plug it in.

It doesn't.

The fan cycles up, blasting an amazing amount of air across

the kitchen.

Mr. Engel moans.

"If you get too cold, I'll turn it off," I say as I return to him. "They don't make them like they used to, right? That thing really moves the air."

The wind makes the closet door bang against its frame. There's an eye hook latch on the outside of the door. I revise my opinion—it wouldn't be a closet door with a latch on the outside. That has to be the door to the cellar, right? Another chill moves through me and I blame the air across my sweaty shirt. Any other thought would be childish.

I laugh at myself and the corners of Mr. Engel's mouth turn up. His eyes are smiling along with me.

"You're feeling a little better, aren't you? Would you like another ice cube?"

I'm still talking way too loud. He has given me no indication that he is hard of hearing. Then again, at his age it would be silly of me to assume otherwise.

I get up again to open the ancient refrigerator. I like the latch on the thing. When it closes, it really locks tight. I wonder why they got rid of those. Before returning to Mr. Engel, I press the cellar door shut with my toe and put the hook through the eye. What a grizzly name for that kind of latch—putting hooks into eyes.

Mr. Engel is watching me do all this with his one good eye. I wonder if the milky one got a hook through it.

"Can you take this?" I ask, pressing the ice cube into his hand.

His fingers close around it and he grimaces.

"It's cold, huh? See if you can put it to your lips. I'm going to look for the ambulance. I'm afraid they might have gotten confused and gone right by your house."

(I would have heard them.)

I would have heard them.

The front door was wide open this whole time and there was no sound until I turned on the fan. I would have heard any vehicle rolling down the dirt road. Over at my uncle's house, I swear that you can hear traffic a mile off. The sound is so out of place.

At night, when we would sit on the deck on the roof of the barn, Uncle Walt would swear that he could hear the highway in the distance. I never could. I think he was making it up. I wish I was there now—back at Uncle Walt's.

I came up here to clean the place out so I wouldn't feel bad about putting it on the market. I couldn't bear the thought of giving up the place before I went through all of Uncle Walt's possessions. There might be something in there that he really treasured and forgot to put in his will. A more insightful person might be able to understand what that means. Am I worried about my own legacy? I don't want to be forgotten after I die—is that why I'm so concerned about what Uncle Walt left behind?

Surely he doesn't care at this point. Whether or not one believes in an afterlife, I'm almost certain that the dead are able to leave behind their earthy concerns.

"How long has it been?" I whisper.

My phone doesn't have the answer. The phone call I tried to make earlier isn't recorded on my list of recent calls—I guess because there was no signal? So, I know what time it is *now*, but not how long I've been waiting.

"Ten more minutes," I say to myself. "Then I'll figure out what to do."

It would take me nearly twenty minutes to get to town and I figure they've been on the road for at least half that. And don't they have, like, volunteers who live throughout the community and respond to calls? I would think that maybe someone from Prescott Road is already headed this way.

I hear a thump from the kitchen.

(He's looking better.)

He's looking better.

In fact, he's up on one elbow for a second. When I come through the doorway, he lowers himself back to the floor.

"That's a good idea. Save your strength," I say. In the brief time that I was away, I missed the fan. Back at my uncle's house, I have the modern equivalent, but it's not nearly as good. With sharp metal blades and virtually no guard in front of it, Mr. Engel's fan turns out a ton of cool air.

I glance around the kitchen with fresh eyes. There is *nothing* in the room that suggests the twenty-first century. There's no microwave, coffee maker, or even a clock over the window that plays birdsong on the hour. Uncle Walt has one of those—that's why I'm thinking about it. Everything in Mr. Engel's house is from the sixties or earlier. They could film movies in here.

The ice cube is a few feet away from Mr. Engel's hand. There's already a decent puddle around it on the vinyl floor.

"You really stuck to your lane, huh?"

I pick up the ice cube and return to him. Settling down to my knees again, I remember the thump.

"Did you have a fall or something while I was in the other room?"

He offers no explanation.

I should get a new piece of ice, but I'm tired of getting up and down. He doesn't seem to mind. He likes it when I put it against his lips.

"There you go."

I whip around when I hear the thump again. It's the cellar door, banging against the frame. The hook is dangling—no longer through the eye.

"Your fan is strong," I say, but I'm doubting the idea even

as the words leave my lips. There's no way that the wind from the fan managed to bang the door enough to free the latch. That would be crazy. Either I imagined latching it, or someone undid it when I left the room. Who, though?

"You didn't get up, did you?" I ask him.

He manages to shake his head.

I turn my body so I can hold the ice against his lips and also keep an eye on the door.

It's just as unlikely that the latch was released by someone from the cellar. The door opens out. How would they get at the latch?

When I hear the bang from the front of the house, a little yelp escapes me.

I squeeze the ice cube so hard that it shoots up and out of my hand, skittering to a stop just in front of the cellar door.

"Paramedics," a voice yells. "Did you call 9-1-1?"

I exhale.

"They're here."

(It's a relief.)

It's a relief.

Even though they're asking me lots of questions, I'm immediately relieved of all responsibility. My part in this story is insignificant. Everything I know about the situation can be conveyed in two sentences. "I came into check on him and found him on the floor of the kitchen. I rubbed ice on his lips."

They ask him a lot of yes or no questions. Their voices are even louder than mine was. I guess they assume that a person is deaf until they are corrected. Mr. Engel never corrects them. He's loaded onto a stretcher and whisked through the house.

I'm allowed to ride in the ambulance if want to.

"No, thank you, that's my truck," I say.

Only then, it occurs to me that I have no business

accompanying him anyway. I'm not even confident that I know his real name.

"You know what, I'm going to see if he has an address book or something. I'll see if I can find a relative who should be notified," I say.

"That would be nice of you," the man says.

They roll out fast, leaving me on the porch.

I watch the cloud of dust on the road. It just hangs in the air. There's no wind to disperse it, so it remains frozen in time. That's like Mr. Engel's house, I suppose.

I pause at the doorway, having second thoughts. It was presumptuous to go into his house the first time, but the door had been open and I had heard a moan. It seems even more rude to go in a second time. What am I going to do, rifle through his possessions looking for a phone number?

"Yup," I say.

I wish the paramedics had stuck around a little longer. Even better, I wish I had asked Mr. Engel who to call on his behalf.

"He'll do that," I say to myself.

As soon as he's feeling a little better, I'm certain that they'll ask him who to call. Old people know phone numbers, right? I would be hard pressed to come up with one, but I'm sure Mr. Engel has at least one phone number at his disposal. If not, the police will probably come over and do an official search for his address book, right? Who am I kidding, they won't have to. They'll be able to track down his next of kin.

I actually turn and start back towards my truck. The sun is searing.

The sun beats down on me as I slow to a stop. I'm running away. It's that simple. The old man, delirious from the heat, has gotten into my head. It was a creepy situation. I shouldn't be ashamed of that. However, I *should* be ashamed that I'm giving up before I notify his relatives that he is on the way to the hospital. It could be hours or days before he's lucid enough to tell them who to call.

My shoulders slump and I turn back around.

I'm not going to let some childhood fear from twenty years ago stop me from doing the right thing, am I?

Then again, isn't this how things always go wrong in the movies? You ignore a gut feeling and then you're doomed.

(Upstairs is even hotter.)

Upstairs is even hotter.

It feels like I'm moving through superheated fluid that burns me as I walk. I can only take tiny sips of air. The dust upstairs smells like it's roasting.

Mr. Engel's address book is on a telephone table next to his dresser. I grab it and try to keep my eyes to myself. I'm doing him a favor, but it was an unrequested favor. It wouldn't be right to let my eyes wander.

He keeps a very tidy bedroom.

A comb and a brush are aligned perfectly on his dresser. The seams of the summer quilt are parallel with the edges of his bed. A pair of shoes and a pair of slippers are tucked under a bench. My uncle had a similar bench next to his closet. It put him a little closer to the floor so he could tie his shoes more easily.

In Mr. Engel's closet, the shirts hang on one side and the pants on the other.

I shut the closet door.

"What am I doing?" I whisper. Sweat is pouring off of me. Any longer and I'll run out of sweat. Mr. Engel will find my mummified remains when he finally comes home.

I'm almost out the door when I remember one more thing.

"The fan," I say, snapping my fingers. I turn for the kitchen. "That thing will burn the place down if I leave it running."

The sign over the bar says, "Work is the curse of the drinking class." I point at it and nod as I pass.

Wiping my fingers first, and then pinching the plug delicately, I work it loose from the outlet and the fan spins down without shocking me. I might as well mop up the puddle from the ice cube with the dish towel, too. With those things done, the kitchen is back in order. I hang the towel over the edge of the sink to dry.

The hook is no longer through the eye.

I stand there, blinking at it and trying to remember.

I latched the door to the cellar twice, didn't I?

This time, I listen to my gut. Without turning my back on that cellar door, I break for the doorway and I don't slow down until I'm out on the porch. Holding my breath and clenching my teeth, I shoot a hand back inside and pull the front door shut. I don't leave it partway open, like Mr. Engel had it.

That house is closed up tight.

Home

(I'm very proud of myself.)

I'm very proud of myself.

Back at home—I've decided to call it "home" instead of "Uncle Walt's house"—I sit down and play detective. The fans are spinning full blast and the Mountain of Pure Rock is supplying a solid block of Aerosmith.

Mr. Engel's address book is flat on the table in front of me.

The reason that I'm proud of myself is because I have deduced a clever way of determining which of the phone numbers might be valid.

The older entries are written in pen with a steady hand. Some of those are just a name and four digits. Back when Uncle Walt moved in, you only had to dial four digits for a local number. The more shaky the handwriting, the newer the entry. I figure that if I'm going to find a living relative, it will be one of the penciled in numbers that's hard to read. Also, friends and businesses are listed with a first and last name. I find the family in the E section, but no last name is listed.

I tap my temple and smile.

"E is for Engel. I knew all that education was going to pay off one day."

The radio reminds me that I'm listening to the Muh-Muh-Muh-Mountain of Pure Rock.

I lean way back in my chair and pull open the refrigerator door so I can grab the soda that I stashed in the crisper. Uncle Walt's refrigerator is practically brand new compared to Mr. Engel's. Uncle Walt wasn't sentimental about appliances, except his washer and dryer. Those things are both thirty years old, at least. They're simple, white, and perfectly functional.

In the E section, I find entries for Greg, Denise, and Amber. My finger pauses under Amber. Her number is mostly fours, eights, and twos. In Mr. Engel's handwriting, those digits are the most discernible. If I have to try Greg, I'll be guessing between threes and fives.

The phone rings and I plug my other ear against the noise of the fan.

I talk to Amber for a couple of minutes. At the beginning of the call, she sounds suspicious that I'm trying to sell her something. It gets awkward again when I don't know where they actually took him. She gets on top of her emotions and manages to thank me several times. Then, she's off to make arrangements for one of the family members to come visit. I tell her to stop by if she makes the trip. She politely blows off that invitation.

I never found out where she lives or how she's related. I didn't even find out Mr. Engel's first name.

When I close the address book, it crosses my mind that I should put it back where I found it.

I laugh out loud, tilting my head back towards the ceiling.

"No, thank you," I say.

There's no mailbox to drop the address book in, so I'll probably put it in a big envelope and mail it back to Mr. Engel. I don't even plan on slowing down the next time I pass his house.

The Mountain of Pure Rock starts to play a Beach Boys song and I raise my eyebrows and nod appreciatively. Before it can get to the chorus, there's a sound a needle scratching across a record and they blast Metallica at me.

I sigh.

(How do you know what to throw away?)

How do you know what to throw away?

I've always lived fairly unencumbered. When I was growing up, Mom and I moved around several times. She never had a great reason, as far as I could tell. The grass is always greener I suppose. It would be the middle of summer and she would come home with pictures or pamphlets of some place that was a few hundred miles away.

"Doesn't it look wonderful?" she would ask.

Nobody would put out a pamphlet for a place that didn't make it look wonderful. They don't photograph the dirty grocery store with the water-stained ceiling and dusty shelves. They wouldn't write about how the police have given up trying to keep the drug dealers away from the elementary school. Tourist pamphlets lie, and they're not meant to entice people to move to a place anyway. They're meant to get you to spend a vacation hiking up to the top of Mount Syphilis, or whatever. That's not something a local person would ever do anyway.

But that's what she would use to try to get me excited about an upcoming move.

I have to admit that I was always pretty willing to move regardless. A move to a new neighborhood and a new school is like a fresh start. I wouldn't have to worry about the bad impression that I had made with the principal of the old school. I wouldn't have to worry about the fact that I had shoplifted from the drug store and wasn't allowed to go in there anymore.

We tossed most everything—furniture, clothes I had grown out of, and toys that I didn't play with—and we moved. This happened several times when I was growing up.

I took that family tradition and kept it going after I graduated from college and lived on my own. I would work in some generic cubicle for a company that did whatever. Then, a couple of years later, I would pick up and go to the next place. It wasn't until Kimberly that I felt the need to put down roots and build a life in a place. That was over in New York. When she died, I was set adrift again.

Now, I don't know what to throw away and what to keep.

My uncle kept all this stuff, so he must have thought that he would want it one day. He had VHS tapes of how to train a colt. As far as I know, he had never trained a colt. Maybe he was planning to one day. I toss them out since I got rid of the VCR on the last trip to the dump.

He had a stack of Fine Furniture magazines. Each one was tabbed with sticky notes that had little messages to himself.

"For the foyer," he wrote about a blanket chest.

I'm not sure whose foyer he meant. His house—*my* house—doesn't have a foyer. The front door, that I have never seen used, opens to the living room. The side door opens to the kitchen. If you come in through the shed, you are in the back of the pantry.

"Foyer," I say. I toss the magazine in the recycle bin.

I could throw everything away, I suppose.

Nobody will ever care about any of this stuff. All the memories associated with this place are going to die with me. I don't have anyone to pass them along to. Uncle Walt never had any kids. Me and my mom were the last of his family. Now, it's just me.

I lean back against the wall. I'm surrounded by piles of memories, trying to decide which ones to discard. I don't have to make the final decision tonight. For the moment, I'll get rid of anything that doesn't resonate with me personally. Uncle Walt is dead. His plans for a blanket chest should be buried too. I keep the magazine that has plans for a weathervane. That's something that I was going to help him build. He taught me how to weld and hammer metal into different shapes. We discussed the most appropriate symbol for his farm. In the end, we decided that the weathervane should be two animals rearing up on their hind legs, like you might see on a coat of arms. I said it should be a horse and a deer. Uncle Walt had wanted a pig and a ram. We had settled on horse and ram. He already started to pound his ram out of a sheet of copper. I drew the outline of my horse, but I haven't cut it out yet. The magazine will tell me how to make the base and the swivel.

That one, I keep.

I've had enough sorting for the night. All the windows are open so the cold air might infuse the house while I sleep. I walk around, making sure the doors are locked and lights are out.

Uncle Walt never locked the doors.

I stop and look through the kitchen window. Everything is perfectly still out there in the moonlight. It would be a good night to go up to the deck on top of the barn and look at the stars. That's the kind of thing that should be shared with someone else though. I'm afraid that if I go up there alone, I won't know what to do with the odd thoughts that occur up there. If you have someone to share them with, they aren't so frightening.

In the distance, I hear the train whistle.

"Nope," I say.

I close all the windows on the first floor and lock them.

(The night is long.)

The night is long.

It seems to get hotter and hotter throughout the night. When I wake up at three, I'm covered in sweat and the moonlight coming through the window is so bright that I swear I can feel the heat on my skin.

Uncle Walt's last bedroom in this house was down on the first floor. There was a period of time there, just before the end, when he couldn't use the stairs reliably. He had his bed set up in the dining room. After he died, I moved it back upstairs. I offered to come stay with him, but he wouldn't hear of it.

"I'm sure you have plenty more important things to do," he

would always say.

Back then, I was lying to him. I was lying to myself, too. I always thought that things might turn around any second. In reality, my career had been over for a while. I never thought that Uncle Walt would die. He was always the strongest person I knew.

I wonder if that's how Amber thinks of Mr. Engel.

Of course, as soon as his name pops into my head, I remember the hook and eye. That cellar door refused to stay shut. It must have been something odd about the framing of the house. There's probably a twist in the doorframe that puts pressure on the door and makes the hook wander out of the eye.

Yes, I know. These are the kind of things that one tells oneself at 3am. In a movie, this type of denial inevitably leads to death. But what's the alternative? Even if I admit that there might have been a murderer down in the cellar, how would they have unlatched the hook from the eye from the other side of the door? To do something like that, they would have to be a *supernatural* murderer. If something like that exists, then there's no sense in fearing it.

Hear me out.

It makes sense to fear and take precautions against an axe murderer or a serial killer because those are the types of threats that someone might defeat. But if there really are vampires down in Mr. Engel's cellar, and they really can unhook latches from the wrong side of the cellar door, then what's the point in fearing them? How can I survive a monster who possesses telekinesis? Being afraid of vampires is like being afraid of asteroids. You're going to die whether or not you acknowledge their existence, but at least ignorance is blissful.

Unless.

Unless vampires are very territorial and I could just move away.

My original plan was to clean out Uncle Walt's place and then sell it. It's only the last day or two that I've considered maybe moving here permanently.

Perhaps that's the decision I have to make.

If I want to stay, then I should deal with the vampires.

If I decide to move, then the vampires can be a problem for the next owners.

I laugh in the darkness and get out of bed.

I need one of the downstairs fans.

(I guess I always liked the strangeness.)

I guess I always liked the strangeness.

One thing I always hated when I was a kid was how my mom was always telling me that I was wrong. It's like with the neighbor and the trashcans—even after Matt and I brought home the foot, she never really apologized even though I had been right all along.

She said something like, "You could have been seriously hurt. Don't you dare do anything like that again."

He was a murderer living right across the alley.

"That's a matter for the police. You shouldn't have gotten involved."

But she wouldn't believe me when I tried to tell her. How were the police supposed to get involved when my own mother wouldn't listen?

"Listen," she said, "Am I glad that he has been apprehended? Yes. Am I glad that you involved yourself? No! Next time, no sneaking."

We never saw eye to eye about that incident. Not once.

For me, the world was full of ghosts, strange phenomena, killers, and UFOs. From my mother's point of view, I had an overactive imagination and a lot to learn about the world.

It wasn't like that at Uncle Walt's place. He knew that the world was a strange place and he didn't shy away from any part of it.

One time, my mom and I were visiting him in the winter. It

was between Thanksgiving and Christmas. Mom got us really cheap plane tickets somehow and we had used them for a mini-vacation. Sitting around the little table in the kitchen one night, the light above the table had flickered.

"Something wrong with your bulb, Walt?" Mom asked.

He put a finger to his lips and pointed at the light over the sink. This time, the light over the table stayed constant but the light over the sink flickered. It was the same pattern—blink, blink, pause, blink. Next, he pointed at the lights in the living room. My chair legs squeaked on the floor when I whipped my body around to watch. The lights in the living room flickered in exactly the same way.

"For heaven's sake, Walt, your wiring is so bad that this place is going to burn down one day."

Uncle Walt waited for the light show to finish before he responded.

"After it's done in the den, it moves upstairs. I've chased it a few times," he said. He took a sip of his hot chocolate. He made it from scratch with real cream. It was as addictive as heroin.

"Get a qualified electrician out here," Mom said.

Uncle Walt shook his head. "I haven't decided if it's fairies, sprites, or maybe aliens. It's some kind of visitor and it seems to be harmless enough."

He pointed to me. "Just remember, foreign and hostile are not synonymous. Don't judge before you know a thing's nature. Stay vigilant, but don't be xenophobic."

"What's xenophobic?" I asked.

"Fear of the unknown," Uncle Walt said. "Some people will simplify it down to fear of foreigners, but it's actually fear of the foreign. That's more than just people from another country."

"It's an *electrical* problem, Walt. Stop messing with my son."

Walt shook his head. "I'm not messing with anyone. If it happens again, I'll prove it to you."

I forgot all about the flickering lights until the last night of our mini-vacation. We were going to leave for the airport in the morning and Mom was sweating out a looming storm. She was afraid that our flight would be cancelled and we would be stranded in Maine. Uncle Walt was completely calm. He said that the weather report was always wrong in the beginning of December.

"They've figured out a lot of things, but December weather in Maine will always be a mystery..."

Mom was about to say something when the lights above the table flickered.

Uncle Walt jumped up from his chair and sprinted for the cellar door. Throwing it open, he practically threw himself down the stairs. A moment later, every light in the house went off. The record player spun to a stop as the music faded.

"Walt, what on earth are you..."

The light over the sink flashed. It was the same pattern, only reversed. Instead of blink, blink, pause, blink, it was flash, flash, pause, flash.

I jumped when I heard my uncle's voice in the darkness.

"See?" he asked.

The flashing moved to the living room.

"Every breaker in the house is off," he said. "Whatever is making those lights flash isn't coming from Central Maine Power."

"It could still be an electrical problem," Mom said. "In fact, I imagine this just means it's even *more* serious."

In the years since, I've studied electricity enough to believe that Mom was wrong. Walt didn't have a generator or any batteries hooked up to his power. There was no good explanation for why the lights flashed at all, let alone in a pattern that roved through the house. Uncle Walt could have hooked up an elaborate system to trick us into believing that there were fairies in his house, but that wasn't in his nature. He wasn't a trickster like that.

His house and his life were just strange—that's one of the things that I liked best about visiting. In other parts of the world, people call you silly or dumb for believing in weird things. At

Uncle Walt's house, you would have to be dumb to *not* believe. If it's all around you, it's undeniable.

The next time we came back for a visit, I asked about the lights.

Uncle Walt shrugged and waved and told me that whatever had been causing the flicker had simply moved on. As quickly as the mysteries arrived, they moved on. Oh well. But there was always something new to wonder at. One time we saw the northern lights over the hills, rolling across the sky. One winter we saw footprints that led from the side door, David's door, out into the snow that disappeared after exactly thirteen paces.

Uncle Walt never tried to come up with dismissive, rational explanations. We experienced what the house offered and sometimes we even investigated, but we never jumped to any conclusions. Most people feel the need to classify and explain. Uncle Walt accepted things as they were.

There's a dark side to that philosophy though. The dark side is that when it's the middle of the night and you can't sleep because of the hook and eye latch at the neighbor's house, you have to accept that there might be telekinetic vampires down in the man's cellar.

If they're over there, they might decide to stroll down the road to my house. After all, Mr. Engel is at the hospital now. If they were feeding on him, they're probably pretty hungry by now.

I'm moving through the dark living room, trying to find the fan. I really don't want to turn on the light and advertise that someone is home. If anything is out there moving around in the dark, I would rather have them assume that this house is still unoccupied.

Then again, telekinetic vampires can probably track someone by their scent. I'm sure I left my scent all over Mr. Engel's house and it's probably coming off of this house in thick waves. If they're out there, they're probably headed my direction.

My hands find the fan and I trace the cord back to the wall so I can unplug it.

At the bottom of the stairs, I stop to look through the window, across the meadow.

When I was a kid, Uncle Walt used to keep the field mowed short. One spring he ran over a family of baby rabbits. After that, he only cut the field in the fall. He called it "bushwhacking" the field, because it would be grown up with heavy brush and seedlings by the time he cut it.

"Around here," he said, "the forest is always encroaching. If you let that field go for two summers, it would be impossible to clear. Not *impossible,* but you know what I mean."

I did know. Together, we had cleared space for a garden behind the manure shed. It had taken forever. The black alders were so thick back there and we had to pull each clump with the big tractor.

The tall grass was pretty in the summer. It would wave in the slightest breeze and I always thought about little rabbit parents, free to raise their babies now that nobody bushwhacked the meadow until fall. Unfortunately, it was also terrific cover for whatever might try to sneak up on the house. Across that meadow and down the road, Mr. Engel's house sat in the dark. The cellar door was open because the hook was out of the eye. Anything that came up from the cellar could track me here and invisibly move through the tall grass of the meadow.

I like the strangeness of Uncle Walt's house and the idea that anything is possible here, but it's not a comforting thought at three in the morning.

I take the fan upstairs.


```
(Everything seems clearer in the morning.)
```


Everything seems clearer in the morning.

Overnight, the heat has broken and the air has that crisp edge that Maine is famous for. I think that's why people like to vacation up here so much. If you come and stay for a couple of weeks, even in the armpit of summer, you're going to wake up at least once to a morning where you can see your breath. Maine wants to remind you that the winter nights are dark and deep. August is only two months away from the first snowfall.

That contrast—between the heat of the noon sun and the chill over the overnight—reminds you that you have to cherish each moment of hot weather. It will soon be gone.

I cherish the cooler air as I come downstairs and survey the mess. I tie up trash bags and take them out to the truck. I bring down a heavy hand on some of the items that had been wavering between the keep pile and the toss pile. It feels good to make bold decisions. It feels right.

In an hour, I have most of the garbage in the back of the truck and the house is looking austere and clean.

I sit down with my coffee and listen to the Mountain of Pure Rock while I go through Uncle Walt's ledger. He recorded all the expenses of the house for decades. Unfortunately, he used his own names for each of the recipients of his checks. It's a bit of a guessing game as I try to align the entries in his ledger to cancelled checks I found in the bottom drawer of his desk. All I'm trying to do is track down a few mysterious expenses that occurred every month, according to his records. I'm terrified that I will fail to pay one of the bills and invite a lien on the house or get one of the services disconnected.

We're listening to Jethro Tull this morning, which is followed by CSN&Y.

The phone rings.

I reach back and grab the cordless phone from the counter.

"Hello?"

I sit up straight when I hear her voice.

After reestablishing our identities, I can already guess what she's going to say by the tone of her voice.

"He passed during the night," Amber says.

"Oh, I'm so sorry."

I want to ask questions, but that would be rude. She answers a couple of them anyway.

"Aplastic anemia, is what they're guessing, although it also could have been just a vitamin deficiency. We're not asking for more tests. He was ninety-seven."

I swallow. All things considered, I think he was doing pretty good for ninety-seven. He was living on his own and climbing those stairs every day. That's not nothing. I don't say any of this. She doesn't need to hear my assessment of a man that I knew for ten minutes.

"There's a tiny, tiny chance that there was something toxic in his house, but if that's true he was probably exposed for decades. I just wanted to mention in case you want to get some blood work done."

"Oh. Thank you."

"No, thank *you*. I'm so glad he didn't, you know... All alone in that house. He loved that house. We could never get him to leave for even a long weekend."

My Uncle Walt was the same way. One time I mentioned an eclipse to him. He said, "Well, if you can get them to have it at my house, I'll be happy to watch it."

She thanks me again for being a nosy neighbor and we say our goodbyes. After we hang up, I almost want to call back. I should have told her to stop by if she comes to clean out the place. I might have some pointers for someone coming to clean out Mr. Engel's house. My experience in that department is super fresh.

I'm just about to pick up the phone when it rings.

It's her again.

"Sorry. I meant to ask you one more thing."

"Yes?"

"Is there any chance—and feel free to say no—but is there a chance you would be willing to stop by the house and shut off the power and water and lock the place up?"

"I'd be happy to, but may I ask why?"

"We're not sure when we're going to get up there and I hate to think of some electrical problem burning the house down or a leaking pipe flooding the place, you know?"

"Yeah, I hear you. The problem is that without heat, the pipes are definitely going to freeze in a couple of months, and if the furnace is anything like the one here, it needs power to keep going."

"Oh," she said.

I'm wondering if she's really young, or maybe lives in an apartment. The issues I'm raising seem pretty obvious, but maybe that's just because I'm living with them right now in Uncle Walt's place. When I was thinking about cleaning out and selling this place, the realtor I talked to warned me that I would need to "pickle" the place for the winter.

"What would you recommend?" she asks.

I tell her the things that my realtor mentioned to me—draining the pipes and adding antifreeze to the toilets and traps. I can hear her brain overloading over the phone.

"You don't have to make these decisions today," I say. "Listen, I'll go over and shut off the power. That will take care of the water too, by the way. The house has a pump."

"Oh?"

Even that seems like too much information for her to process.

"Don't sweat it," I say. "Just make a note on your calendar to think about this again in a month or so, okay?"

"Okay," she says. She sounds relieved. A month is far enough away that she can catch her breath. "Thanks again."

I don't mention the thing about stopping by. I'll bring it up when we talk again, if we ever do. I'm starting to think that Amber is never going to set foot in Mr. Engel's house. I want to ask how she's related, but I hold that question too. It will likely be answered by the obituary.

We say our goodbyes and hang up.

It's not until I put the phone back in the charger that I realize what I've just signed up for.

"Turn off the power," I say with a sigh.

I'm thinking about Uncle Walt's breaker box. It's located in the cellar. I bet Mr. Engel's is too.

Cellar

I have put it off as long as I dare.

Now, it's about five in the afternoon. I still have three hours until sunset.

I did every other errand and chore I could think of first. I went grocery shopping and got my hair cut. By the way, it only costs six dollars to get a crew cut around here. Any other cut costs ten. I think it's Mr. Bean's way of imposing his sensibility on the men of the area. I replaced two of the tires on the truck as well. The rear tires were brand new and the old were circulated to the front. The spare was back in the bed.

I have no more excuses.

I drive the truck down the road and park it in Mr. Engel's driveway. The crisp air from the morning has all burned away. We are back in the heat and I am staring at Mr. Engel's front door from the driver's seat.

The Mountain is playing a song by Elton John. I shut off the radio and push open the driver's door as a breeze stirs.

I sing to myself under my breath as I look at the house. "Hey, kids, shake it loose together."

If this was a western, this would be the showdown in the

center of town. Me out in front of the saloon, flipping my keys around a finger—the house down near the jailhouse, waiting for me to draw.

But this isn't a western, it's a horror movie. This is the part where you yell at the screen while the hapless hero goes into the house against everyone's better judgement.

When I take a step forward, the breeze pushes open the front door a little.

"Come on," I whisper.

This is too much. I know that I closed the door. I didn't lock it because I figured that Mr. Engel might not have his keys, but I *know* that I closed it.

Someone must have been here in the interim. Maybe the police finally came by to check out the place? I could come back another day. I could just break my promise to Amber. What does it matter if the power is shut off? Then again, what's stopping me? Some childish fear caused by an absurd declaration from a dying man?

I climb the porch and put my toe on the door to push it open, just like yesterday.

"Hello?" I call.

I immediately regret yelling into the empty house. The way my voice reverberates back is chilling, even in the late afternoon heat.

I remember Mr. Engel and his one good eye. The poor old man has passed now. This house was important to him—so much so that he wanted nothing more than to pass his final days here alone. I step inside. The heat is oppressive, but not nearly as bad as it was yesterday. I glance around, making sure the windows are shut tight. Amber didn't ask me to do that, but it only makes sense.

Work is the curse of the drinking class. I take the soiled glass from the bar and walk it into the kitchen. The dishtowel is dry now. I put it back on the stove handle, where I found it in the first place. When I rinse out the glass, washing the brown stain out with my fingers, the pipes groan and chatter before they deliver water.

I check the rest of the windows on the first floor before I even dare to look at the cellar door.

The hook is out of the eye.

From my back pocket, I pull out the little flashlight that I bought at the grocery store. It was in the "Seasonal" aisle, right next to the bug spray and sunscreen. In my other pocket, I have a box of matches. I have zero intention of going down there without adequate light.

I reach out and tug on the door, letting it swing open while I back up.

I stab at the darkness with my flashlight beam.

My mom hated spiders. Every time she came to visit Uncle Walt, they had a fight about it. She would take the old broom out to the side porch and sweep away all of the webs and the fat spiders that built them. Within a day, we wouldn't be able to sit out there in the evenings—there would be too many mosquitoes and biting flies.

"You can just put on bug spray, like a normal person," she would say.

"Great, we'll just add poison to the equation. That's far better than a few helpful spiderwebs," Uncle Walt would say.

I'm guessing that Mr. Engel and my mom would have gotten along. I don't see a single spiderweb in the open framing of the stairway leading down to his cellar. He didn't coddle the spiders. My flashlight barely finds any dust either. The whole stairwell is remarkably clean. I point my flashlight down and study the well-worn stairs. Each tread has a shallow depression right in the middle. These boards have seen a lot of use through the years.

The light switch turns on a bulb just over my head and one at the bottom of the stairs. I keep my flashlight on anyway. Once I kill the power to the house, I'll need it.

I take a step down.

This is where a hand will shoot out from between the treads and grab my foot. Or, maybe all the treads will tilt down, turning the staircase into a ramp. Either would be terrifying.

The song from the Mountain is still in my head.

"We'll kill the fatted calf tonight, so stick around," I whisper.

It was the wrong lyric to remember when I'm trying to psych myself up to descend into a vampire-infested cellar.

(What if vampires were real?)

What if vampires were real?

I'm a big believer in self-ownership, you know? As long as they're not harming someone else—directly or indirectly—I believe that a person should be able to do what they like. Of course, the devil is in the details. If I choose to commit suicide and someone else really cares for me, then I'm harming them, right? Should I be allowed to do it anyway?

Are animals people? Should I be able to harm an animal? We have a ton of rules about that. You can kill a cow and eat it, but you had better not inflict too much pain on the poor thing while the heart is still pumping.

I eat meat, but I try not to be a hypocrite about it. I don't shy away from pictures and videos of cows and pigs being slaughtered. In my opinion, if you morally object to watching an animal being slaughtered, then you probably don't have any business eating it.

Kimberly used to yell at me all the time about such things. She would never, *ever*, allow herself to witness an animal bleeding. She also wouldn't watch a rabbit being skinned. Neither of those things ever kept her from enjoying a ribeye though.

"People are omnivores," she would remind me. "But it's sick to take pleasure from watching something else die."

"Is that why you took a picture of your salmon steak before you ate it?" I asked.

That wasn't a real argument. We were only teasing each other. We didn't have that many real arguments.

Back to vampires—what would we do if they were real?

Polar bears hunt people, right? Mountain lions will sometimes kill a jogger. Sharks certainly don't have any compunction about munching on a swimmer. We don't go around trying to eradicate those species just because they predate on humans.

If vampires were real, would we respect their right to survive, or would we try our best to snuff them all out? What if they existed, but the lore was all wrong? In our fiction, vampires are created by converting a human. In some books and movies, a single bite is enough to infect a person and doom them to feast on blood. If one thinks about it that way, then vampirism is akin to a disease and we certainly don't have any prohibition on trying to eliminate diseases.

The other thing that Kimberly and I used to debate was the death penalty. She thought I was a hypocrite about that too, but I thought that my stance was remarkably consistent. I view the death penalty with the same point about self-ownership. Let's say, in a fit of rage, you murder someone. You've violated someone else's right to live. What should be the punishment? Ideally, we would be able to permanently eject you from our society. Since you violated our most sacred rule, you've demonstrated that you don't belong with the rest of us. Unfortunately, we don't have anywhere to send you. Therefore, we cast you off in the only way we know how—death.

Kimberly would argue that education and rehabilitation are possible and therefore should be attempted. Kimberly would argue that the inevitability of a single innocent person being executed should nullify the practice. I don't disagree with either of those ideas, but I think that they are unnecessarily cautious.

Here's where she calls me a hypocrite—as much as I believe in self-ownership, I don't really have a strong opinion about the sanctity of life. In my mind, life just isn't that precious.

"That goes against everything you just said," Kimberly told

me.

And then, less than a year after we had this debate, she was pregnant. My ideas about the sanctity of life began to shift dramatically as I watched her body change and saw the life growing inside her. Then, when she and the baby both died, I understood that my opinions didn't matter at all. People can be ripped right out of our hearts before we even get to see the color of their eyes. We're all connected, for better or worse. Most of the time it's worse.

I take another step down into the cellar.

(It doesn't smell bad.)

It doesn't smell bad.

In fact, it smells just fine. It smells a good bit like Mr. Engel did—like a towel fresh from the dryer. As I take another step down, I see why. His washer and dryer are installed right there at the bottom of the stairs. The house we rented in Virginia was like that. It had a basement laundry as well. I never really understood that. Why would you take your clothes down into the dirtiest room of the house in order to clean them?

The temperature drops a few degrees with each step. The air is dry down here, too. It's not at all what I would have expected. No spiders, no dust, fresh smell, and dry air—Mr. Engel should have set up a little bed down here and spent all of his time in this space. It's a million times more comfortable than upstairs.

Still, I want to get out of here.

I want to find the electrical panel, do what I said I would do, and get home.

There are two bulbs hanging from the ceiling. They do a decent job of lighting up the appliances and the shelves with all their jars. I sweep my flashlight around anyway, examining the concrete foundation, looking for a gray panel.

I'm looking for other things too, but I don't let myself think about that. Are there supposed to be coffins down here? If I had paid attention outside, this process would be easier. I could have noted which side of the house the power line was attached to. I could have spotted where the meter was mounted and where the electrical service entered the house. I didn't do any of those things, so now I'm left to...

"There," I say. My flashlight reflects off the steel screws in the corners of the panel. It looks reasonably new compared to everything else in the house. The washing machine and dryer could be out of a Sears catalog from 1950. The furnace looks like it would have been right at home in the hold of the Titanic. But the electrical panel could be brand new.

Before I focus my full attention on that, I have to make sure. I have to be one-hundred percent sure that there's no truth behind what Mr. Engel said.

My flashlight continues its sweep around the cellar.

I see a couple of big vertical cylinders that I have come to understand have something to do with the water. One is probably a heater and the other stores the water that has been pumped? I don't know for sure. I've mostly been an apartment dweller in my life. We don't deal with that kind of thing. My understanding of basement utilities is just high enough that I'm able to condescend about the knowledge that Amber has of such matters.

I recognize one thing that I see. There's a big freezer tucked under the stairs.

Uncle Walt had one of those too. He used to raise beef. Most of the animals, he sold. He would have one butchered and then freeze the meat in his cellar to use for the winter. Maybe Mr. Engel had a similar arrangement.

If I shut off the power, Amber might have a giant mess of rotted meat to deal with.

"Plus anything in the kitchen," I whisper.

I've seen the upstairs freezer. There was little in that except for ice. It would be kind of me to clean out the fridge though.

I sigh, wondering what I've gotten myself into.

My first inclination is to march back up the stairs, call Amber, and alert her to the food situation.

That's silly. She doesn't need another headache on top of what she's already dealing with. Besides, I don't even know that there's anything in the freezer.

Before I turn off the breakers, I should check.

(There's enough light from the bulb.)

There's enough light from the bulb.

I don't need the flashlight for this. I tuck it in my back pocket and lift the lid on the freezer. It's newer than the fridge upstairs. Instead of a mechanical latch, the lid is only kept in place with a rubber seal. It pops open, breaking the seal reluctantly, and white fog rolls out from inside. The mist is dense in there. I wave my hand to clear it away so I can...

There are eyes looking up at me.

I gasp and the lid slips from my hand. It slams shut as I'm taking a quick step back. With a hand pressed against my chest, I can feel my heartbeat slamming against my ribs. My breath is coming in short bursts. I back up two more steps and nearly trip over my own feet.

Those eyes are burned into my brain.

They were wide and almond-shaped, but I didn't see any white. The pupils were vertical slits, surrounded by deep violet, threaded with lighter purple. I have to admit that the color was probably altered by the dim light from the overhead bulb.

None of that matters though. What matters is getting up the stairs and away from the freezer. My body is so amped up on adrenaline that my legs might as well be a million miles away. They work just fine as they propel me up the stairs at lightning speed. I slam the cellar door shut and press my shoulder against it as my fingers fumble to put the hook into the eye. It's such a feeble mechanism. The latch has already proven more than once its inability to stay locked.

I brace myself against the door as I reach for the phone.

My hand squeezes the receiver in a death grip as my trembling finger stabs into the nine hole. I get it around and wait forever as it dials back to the stop. Then I jerk out one, one.

I try to get ahold of my breathing as the phone clicks and crackles in my ear.

I swear I can feel pressure against the door.

I lean harder into it.

One of my shoes squeaks against the vinyl floor.

"9-1-1 what's your..."

"GET OVER HERE NOW."

There's a pause.

"Help is on the way, sir. Can you tell me the nature of..."

"I'm back at Mr. Engel's. You can get the address from the phone like the other day. There's a body down in the cellar. It's in the freezer."

"Sir? There's a body?"

This is not the angel from the other day. This man sounds mildly interested, but also frustrated at having to assist me. He also sounds like he's about sixteen years old. He has that know-it-all tone of someone who hasn't experienced a damn thing but acts like it's all old hat.

I'm pressing so hard against the door that the wood creaks. I imagine the wood splintering from the pressure, sending me tumbling down the stairs into the darkness.

I pull out the flashlight to have it at the ready. As I repeat myself to the operator.

The line crackles.

My story is a little more detailed this time. I mention Amber and how she asked me to turn off the power. I mention checking the freezer to make sure it's not filled with meat that will spoil. Words tumble from my mouth and into the phone like a frantic confession. I ask how long it will take for help to arrive.

That's when I start to rethink everything.

Why didn't I run? I could be back at Uncle Walt's house right now, having this conversation while I mixed myself a Tom Collins at a safe distance. Instead, I have my ear pressed against the door. Something is moving down there.

I hear a dry scrape of icy flesh against the worn stair treads. Maybe that part is my imagination, or maybe it's just the ancient refrigerator behind me as it fires up. The thump is real though. I don't just hear that—I feel it through the floor.

Static barks down the phone line. I wonder if they still bother to maintain these things. At my uncle's house—my house —the phone eventually plugs into the back of the cable box. Mr. Engel is the only person on this whole road who utilizes the copper phone lines. They might be barely operable.

"Sir?"

"Please come quickly," I whisper.

"Sir, is there someone in the house with you? Are you being threatened?"

Now, I think I understand. A questionable report of a dead body might warrant a low-priority visit from a police officer. They'll probably arrive in forty-five minutes, not even bothering to put on their lights or speed to the scene. I'm just guessing, of course. I'm no expert in emergency response. The other day, people arrived fast, but that was to save Mr. Engel's life.

"Yes," I whisper. "I'm afraid I am."

Perhaps that will light a fire, so to speak.

"Stay on the line," he says. He sounds excited now. The frustration is gone. "We will..."

The phone clicks, goes silent, and then buzzes out a tone.

A thump reverberates through the door.

I ease the phone back into the cradle and shift my weight, pressing my back against the door and bracing my legs against the vinyl floor. This position feels strong, but I'm not sure how long I can hold it.

(Each thump is followed by silence.)

Each thump is followed by silence.

I keep trying to remember what I saw in the freezer. The mist flowing out was clear. Was it cold though? Am I sure that the freezer was actually frozen, or was that mist more of a warm fog? I'm not entirely positive why it makes a difference to me. Whether or not the body was frozen, it was in that confined space and there couldn't have been any oxygen. So how is it on the move now?

More troubling than the temperature of the mist is what was around the body. The head had been really close to the top of the freezer, and that freezer was enormous. There could have been an entire cow's worth of meat in that thing. How many human bodies would fit in a freezer that size? Three? Four? Did I see more bodies stacked below? How many things are climbing the stairs right now?

My legs are beginning to tremble.

The door creaks behind me.

I'm almost certain that the strain on the wood is coming from the other side. I'm not pressing any harder than I was before. This is crazy—everything is going sideways. The last time everything went sideways on me, I wasn't taking things seriously enough and I paid the price.

There might be one perfect thing to do, and I'm determined to figure out what that is.

I need to act like my father.

Here's why I say that: when I was a little kid my mom would get really frustrated or disappointed with me. She would always shake her head, sigh, and say, "You're acting just like your father." That, I knew, was her gravest insult. I had never met my father. The man had been long gone before I was born. From the way she spoke about him, I knew him to be the source of her deepest pain. Therefore, I understood that "acting like my father" meant that I was causing her the deepest possible amount of pain. As a little kid, that was devastating.

I as grew older, I started to realize how unfair she was being. She was flogging me with my own genetics, like it was my decision who she had bred with. The only witness to my father's lack of character was her. I had no way to dispute or even really understand. That's when I decided that it was up to me to interpret the meaning. I decided that my father had been extremely smart and logical. Therefore, "acting like my father" was the highest compliment.

I need to act like my father.

There may or may not be something in the cellar, pressing against the other side of a thin door with a weak latch. It may or may not be a monster that was lifeless in the freezer until I woke it up. The police may or may not be rushing to my rescue.

When the phone rings, the sound interrupts my analysis.

I run.

Home

(I make it home by sunset.)

I make it home by sunset.

Technically, it's before sunset, but the sun has descended below the hill. If I'm counting on direct sunlight for safety, that ship has sailed. I'm back in the house with the door slammed behind me before the dust has even settled in the driveway outside. I run from window to window, making sure that everything is shut and locked. This time, I don't stop on the first floor. I close and lock everything upstairs as well. I even lock the hatch that leads up to the attic and close the chimney flue.

In the back of the pantry, a door connects to the shed.

The plank door on the shed—where I park the tractor—slides shut and I put a padlock through the hasp. David's door is locked. I don't know why Uncle Walt called it David's door. It's probably some inside joke. I continue on to the barn, making sure everything is shut tight before I climb up into the loft and then through the door to the roof deck.

From up there, I can see down the road. I can't see Mr. Engel's entire house, but I can see the tops of the two trees that flank his house. I'm just in time to see the flashing police lights coming down the road. They cut through the amber glow that precedes sunset.

"Good," I whisper. There are two cars. They took me seriously.

I could get the telescope from its case in the barn and get a better look. I play that out in my head—me watching from a distance, isolated and helpless.

This is when the second-guessing starts. Should I call someone? Should I...

"Be there," I say.

I should. I should be there.

Did I tell the operator where the freezer was located? Did I give them my name?

(I pull up and wait.)

I pull up and wait.

It's a strange thing to hope for the worst. A big part of me wants to be vindicated. With the truck's engine still idling and my hand on the gearshift, I almost want to see a bloody figure stagger out from the doorway, proving my panic justified. That would be terrible. How can I wish the worst for someone who has taken a job in service to the community?

I shouldn't just sit here. I should go in and...

"Get shot," I whisper.

Good point. I should definitely *not* go inside unannounced.

I lay my palm on the horn and get ready to signal my arrival.

Two officers come through the front door of Mr. Engel's house. Neither is covered with blood.

One raises a radio and says something.

I shut off the truck. Parked at the end of Mr. Engel's driveway, I'm a good distance away, but not so far that I don't see one of the officers tense up as he regards me. I slow down and he seems to relax a little.

The one on the radio sounds like a woman. I wonder for a moment if she could be the angel who answered my call the other day. I shake away the thought—they wouldn't make officers answer the phones.

"Hi," I call, raising a hand.

The male officer raises his chin towards me. I guess it's a greeting?

"I'm the one who called about the freezer?"

The woman starts towards me. I've seen her before, but I can't think where.

"Did you find it?" I ask.

She takes one more step and I figure it out—she was one of the first people to arrive when Mr. Engel collapsed. She had assessed his condition before the ambulance arrived. In a police uniform, she looks totally different.

"Can you describe what you saw?" she asks.

Unembellished by my imagination, it doesn't take me long to convey the details.

"But I can just show you," I say.

She cuts a glance over to the other officer.

He says, "Why don't you do that."

(They don't share their opinion with me.)

They don't share their opinion with me.

This is the part of a horror movie that always bugs me. There's that part where the protagonist is the only one who understands what's going on and they can't convince anyone else of the danger.

I'm Ellen Ripley, telling the rest of the crew that it's unsafe to let Kane back on board with a face hugger attached to him. I'm Laurie Strode, trying to convince her teenage friends that a really tall gentleman has been following her around all day on October thirty-first. I'm Wendy Torrance, trying to convince her husband that they need to leave the Overlook hotel before the insanity there kills them all.

"Shit," I whisper.

"Sir?" the female officer asks.

I try to smile. "I just realized that in the horror movies, it's always the woman who survives."

Maybe the female officer is the protagonist. She just stares at me.

We're standing above the freezer. It's completely empty. White mist is spilling over the lip. I wave my hand at the vapor.

"Was the door at the top of the stairs latched?" I ask.

"No," she says.

"It was when I left. Maybe the person in here wasn't dead. Maybe I frightened them and they got up and left."

I'm thinking about the thumping on the stairs, but I don't mention it.

"I don't think that door stays latched," she says. "It didn't the other day."

We've had this conversation before. Everything was so hectic with Mr. Engel that I forgot about it. She and I already discussed how the cellar door wouldn't stay latched.

She's staring at me—studying me.

It's amazing how easily a calm person can sweep away my fear. I take a step back from the freezer. To go through the whole story again would be too embarrassing. With no evidence, I'm very aware of how crazy I must seem.

"Look, I'm not going to apologize for calling," I say. "I know that it's impossible for you guys to believe me because there's nothing here that matches what I saw, but I'm certain of what I'm telling you. But I understand. I understand."

I'm backing towards the stairs.

"Can you guys shut off the power before you go? I told Amber that I would and I was about to when I stopped to check the freezer. I'll be at my house if..."

"Wait," the male officer says. He takes out his flashlight and clicks the button. His beam cuts through the mist and into the interior of the freezer.

The two officers lean closer to the freezer.

"Right there," he says.

"Sir?" the female officer says, waving me over.

I'm helpless to disobey her command.

When I get close enough, she reaches out and takes my hand.

Before I can ask what she's doing, she examines my hand front and back and then turns back to the freezer. I see what they're looking at.

"Much smaller," she says.

In the ice buildup on the side of the freezer, we're looking at a handprint. The fingers that left the print are much smaller and more delicate than mine. The female officer leans in even closer. I hear her take a deep breath and hold it before her head breaches the confines of the freezer.

When she comes back up, she says a single word.

"Hair."

They nod to each other.

She turns to me.

"You can go home. Please don't mention this to anyone else. We'll notify you when we've reached a conclusion."

She escorts me out of the cellar.

(It's lonely at home.)

It's lonely at home.

At least I have visual contact with the efforts over at Mr. Engel's house. I see more vehicles pull up. Cars are shuffled. It's hard to tell through the telescope, but I think that the female officer leaves. I'm trying to remember if they said they would turn off the power. It doesn't really matter. I'm not ever going back into Mr. Engel's house. If Amber calls again, I'll just hang up.

Maybe she will sell the place and I'll become friends with the new people who live there.

After hours of people moving in and out of the house, I spot the police rolling a big object around the side of the house and lifting it into a van. I believe that they've impounded the freezer.

It would probably best to *not* be friends with the new people, if any do move into Mr. Engel's house. When I lived in apartments, I always found that it was difficult to be friends with my nearest neighbors. They always know when you're coming and going, so there's an accidental intimacy that doesn't allow any wiggle room. You can't lie and say that you're going to be gone all day if they ask you for a favor. You can't have company over without them wondering why they weren't invited.

Mr. Engel's house is a little too close. Maybe that's why Uncle Walt wasn't really friends with him.

I pull the blanket around my shoulders. It's too warm up on the barn deck, but the blanket helps with the mosquitoes. I adjust my telescope so I can see through the upstairs window. Someone is moving around in Mr. Engel's bedroom. I guess maybe they found more evidence up there.

When the phone rings, I panic and fumble to shut off the sound. The people in the lens of the telescope look close enough that they might hear it.

It's the policewoman. She asks me if I can come in tomorrow and record a statement about what I saw. I ask if I'm in trouble and I immediately regret the question. That's the kind of thing a guilty person would ask, and it's the kind of question that she would ever answer honestly.

"No, of course not. We just would like to get your statement clearly recorded."

I agree. What else would I do?

A couple of years ago, I watched a video posted by a lawyer on why one should never talk to the police. It was a long video— two parts, that I believe ran more than an hour—but it was really interesting. The lawyer had broken down every angle in a way that wasn't scummy at all. It made me realize how technical lawyers are. Perhaps this is obvious to everyone else. I used to think that lawyers were very creative and intuitive. The way that this guy examined his thesis from every possible angle, I began to think of lawyers like physicists. They take a statement or an idea and then they probe it, scientifically, from every possible perspective, looking for weaknesses.

In the end, I had been completely convinced. It is *never* advantageous to talk to police. Any sort of statement can be misconstrued and used against you, regardless of your innocence. Even if you're the person who is making a complaint, you can be cornered and accidentally implicate yourself without even knowing it.

Talking to the officer on the phone just now, I had agreed immediately to come in and make a statement. How dumb is that?

I think that it's because she was there, in the house. I went through a traumatic event and I'm seeking the company of other people who witnessed the same things. It was smart of them to have her call me. I want to talk to her—to find out if she felt the same ominous energy that I did down in that cellar. We had been poking around in a predator's den with the threat that it might return at any second. It was like swimming in the ocean, far from shore, knowing that sharks lurk below.

PART THREE:

SACRIFICE

Visitors

(What was I thinking?)

What was I thinking?

I could have fled. I should have waited for the police to leave Mr. Engel's, packed a getaway bag, and then hit the road. I could be at the Super 8 near the highway, worried about bedbugs instead of holding my breath and staring at the ceiling.

I swear that I just heard a knock downstairs.

There were no headlights, and I definitely didn't hear the sound of a car rolling into my driveway. Uncle Walt has a rubber hose across the driveway. He got it from a service station that went out of business when self-serve gas stations took over. If a car runs over that hose, a loud chime sounds in the house. Even a bicycle can trigger it. So I know that whomever just knocked must have arrived on foot.

Assuming, of course, that I really heard a knock.

It's possible that I was half asleep and the sound was part of a dream.

KNOCK. KNOCK.

I exhale slowly and lower my feet to the floor. There's no denying it this time.

It has to be the police.

I turn on my light and squint until I can see.

They probably found evidence of a dead body and they've moved up my questioning to right now. It's the only explanation that I can live with, so I act accordingly. My shorts are draped over the chair, but I go to the closet instead and grab a pair of jeans. Another knock comes while I'm putting on my socks.

"I'm coming," I whisper. I check myself in the mirror. Unshaven and puffy-eyed, I look a little homeless. Whatever.

I put on every light on my path as I walk through. Moving down the stairs, I realize that I'm already fixing in my imagination what I will find when I open the front door. I'll see two uniformed officers with their hands vaguely near their belts, ready for anything.

They knock again as I'm crossing the living room.

I've never seen this door used—not once. There's a bird feeder hanging out there, but my uncle never even used the front door in order to refill it. Using an old coffee can, he would walk the birdseed around from the side door. My mother asked him one time why he didn't open that door, if at least to get some sunlight and fresh air into the living room. His response was, "Open that door? I might let some of the spiders out."

There's no light out there for me to turn on. I reach for the lock and pause just before I turn the bolt.

"Who is it?"

There's a pause. One second passes, two, three, and then, finally, the visitor knocks two more times. The skin on the back of my neck crawls. My mother would say that someone had walked over my grave. She said that whenever I got goosebumps.

"Who is it?"

This time, there's no response at all. I take a step back from the door, wiping my hands on my jeans. All of a sudden, my palms are sweaty. I've thrown away most of the junk that was piled on the floor in the living room, but there's a trophy next to the garbage can that I haven't been able to get rid of. Uncle Walt won the trophy for backstroke in high school. It's tall and has a thick marble base. I grab it by the gilded body and hold it ready to strike.

Stepping to the right, I angle myself so I can see through the front window at the porch that we never use. The lamp is reflecting off the glass so I click it off.

I see the shadow of a person crouching on the porch, just under the bird feeder. At least I think that's what it is. It could be some sort of animal. My hand is gripping the trophy so hard that the figure's little gold arm is digging into my palm.

The thing freezes. Maybe it senses that I'm watching it. The head swivels up and the eyes fix on me. Even though there's little light falling on it, I can see the eyes. They're reminiscent of eyes that I've seen before. I hold my breath and shuffle forward another step. I want to know—are they the same eyes I saw in the freezer?

Before I can be sure, the thing is sliding away, melting into the dark.

I let out my breath with a shudder.

"It had to be a person," I whisper. "Animals don't knock."

I back slowly towards the kitchen. Before I cross through the doorway, I reach around the wall and flip on the lights. Now, nearly every light on the first floor is on. I rush to the side door and flip on the side porch light as I look down through the window. I'm expecting to see another hunched figure, but the side porch is bare.

After rechecking the lock, I grab the cordless phone.

It won't dial.

At first, I suspect the battery. The cordless phone is old enough that if I leave it off the charger for a few hours, it will die. But it's beeping when I hit the button and the base station clicks on when I press the intercom. There's just no connection to the outside world.

My cellphone is upstairs.

Before retreating, I check the locks. Everything is locked tight—side door, front door, and even the door at the back of the pantry. I leave all the lights on and I peer through every window before I climb the stairs. I have no bars in the house. It's not surprising. The signal is terrible out here and there's a metal roof. Sometimes I can get a signal up on the deck on top of the barn, but not always.

I have wifi though—I can text for help.

My message doesn't go through.

Of course. If the landline is out, that means that my cable connection is down. I have a wifi connection to the router, but the router can't talk to the outside world.

What was I thinking?

(What other choice do I have?)

What other choice do I have?

This isn't a rhetorical question. I'm asking myself as I stand in the pantry, eyeing the door that leads through the shed to the barn. Everything is locked up. I made sure of that last night. All the doors to the outside are locked. I even locked the bulkhead from the inside. All the windows on the first floor are shut and locked and I shut all the upstairs windows when I grabbed my phone.

I'm realizing how silly locks are. You can break a pane of glass accidentally with a baseball—am I really trusting the windows to keep out whatever was knocking on my door?

"No," I whisper. "Trusting the windows is not an option."

The pantry might be a good bet though. It has a solid lock on the door to the shed and I can wedge the door shut from the kitchen. It's an interior room with no windows. Maybe I could barricade myself in here, wait until morning, and then make a run for it.

"Then what?" I ask myself.

Then what... Leave town? Never come back to this place?

Maybe I could stay at the Super 8 and just come back during the day to finish cleaning out the house and then put it on the market. I could live off a credit card for a while, I suppose. It will be a stretch. I might have to list Uncle Walt's house for less than it's worth so I won't get too far into debt, but it's a possible solution.

"All because someone was crouching on the porch?" I whisper.

No. I shake my head. If it was just the knocking and the person crouching, I wouldn't be thinking like this. It's everything. It's Mr. Engel and the freezer. It's the police and the investigation. It's all of that *and* the knocking.

I'm a firm believer in taking the damn hint. It was stupid of me to stay in this house tonight and I'm not going to make that mistake again.

So, what choice do I have?

I'm not going to try to sprint across the dooryard to the truck. That would be stupid. Option one is to barricade myself in the pantry. Option two is to go up to the deck on top of the barn and see if I can get a signal on my phone. The cops will take me seriously this time—I'm sure of it.

I stand there, breathing slowly as I weigh the options. It's such a good phrase—weigh one's options. The two different options do have a distinct weight. The idea of huddling in the pantry weighs heavier on my heart than climbing up to the deck. I hate the idea of hiding here—pathetic and waiting for death to come.

If I'm honest, it's not really a choice. I'm not dumb enough to try to sprint across the dooryard to the truck, and I'm not so timid that I can make myself hide in the pantry all night.

I take a breath and reach for the doorhandle.

"Shoes and keys," I whisper to myself.

Keys—that's a great idea. I'll lock the door behind me so the pantry will be still be a safe spot to retreat to. When I return to the kitchen, I swear I see something dart by the edge of the circle of light outside. It could have been a bat—there are a lot of them out there at night, swooping and snatching all the summer bugs. The bugs bite me and take my blood, then the bats eat the bugs. They're one step removed from subsisting off of my vitality.

My shoes are in the kitchen, next to the door. I slip them on and tie them tight.

I snatch the keys and retreat through the pantry, wedging a broom against the door to the kitchen.

(It feels like quiet safety.)

It feels like quiet safety.

I wonder if all barns feel so secure. Maybe this one just feels so peaceful because I'm remembering the way that it used to be. In the summer, Uncle Walt would bring in the cows, sheep, and goats at night. They would munch on hay and sleep. He had one cow that would snore when it slept. The barn would smell sweet from the hay and grain. The atmosphere always made me sleepy when I would come out to fill the water buckets one more time before bed.

I leave the lights off—no need to advertise my position—and I climb the ladder into the loft. I have to be careful up here. There's a trapdoor over the horse stalls. I shuffle around that and find the short ladder that leads to the hatch in the roof. I push it open, catching it before it can slam down on the deck.

The stars are a dotted blanket above. This would be a perfect night for the telescope. It's still pointed at Mr. Engel's house. The lights are all off over there now. I wonder if the police remembered to turn off the breakers before they left.

Standing on the hatch, I try my phone.

It shows one bar, but I can't get a call to go through.

It's amazing that I have gone my whole life without having to dial 911, and now it has happened so many times in such a short period. I pace the deck, trying to find if the signal is any better. I have one bar and then none. Setting the phone down on the railing makes the bar come back. I try a call on speaker phone. For a moment, it sounds like it's going to ring and then "Call Failed" appears on the display.

I try sending a message and it bounces back immediately.

I climb the railing, lifting my phone high. I know it's a long shot.

With the phone on speaker, extended as high as it will go between my pinched fingers, it starts to ring.

A new sound draws my attention though.

It's the sound of the hatch rising up behind me. I turn and see a hand slip through the gap. The door creaks upwards and I can see the eyes.

As soon as I lock onto them, they're the only thing I see. This is just like Mr. Engel's cellar. Those eyes were so captivating that I didn't get a good look at what else was in the freezer. Now, the rest of the world disappears and my focus is completely dedicated to the subtle glow of the eyes that are emerging from the darkness. Maybe they're just reflecting the starlight, but I don't think so. I think that they have their own internal source of light, and that light pulses, synchronizing perfectly with my thoughts.

I'm aware of my cellphone tumbling from between my fingers and then disappearing below.

My rigid body is balanced on top of the railing as a head pushes the trapdoor out of the way and the second hand emerges from below. It's in the shape of a human, but hesitate to describe it as a person. It's staying close to the ground, moving almost like a spider as it pulls its way through the hatch.

I'm swaying slightly. Even with no conscious control of my muscles, my body wants to stay upright, but the railing isn't cooperating. It has picked up a sway beneath my feet as my legs adjust to compensate.

The figure slips its last foot through the hatch and the door falls shut behind it. Now, it's rising up on its legs. The hands are reaching for me. My eyes are still locked onto its eyes. They pulse and glow. They're violet with veins of lighter purple through each iris.

When the lips part, I see that the teeth must be glowing too.

My foot slips, and I fall.

(The fall is a blessing.)

The fall is a blessing.

Sense returns to me as soon as the fall breaks my eye contact. I hit the shingles and roll. The whole front part of the house is clad in a metal roof. The barn and the shed are all shingles. It's a good thing, too—I think that a slippery metal roof would have ushered me quickly towards the ground.

Instead, I scrape a patch of skin from my arm, roll over and skid to a halt a dozen feet below the deck. I can hear it up there, moving around on the planks. It makes a hissing sound. When I glance in that direction, I see its hand extend over the side of the deck and I look away quickly before its eyes can capture me again.

In my mind, I construct a quick map of my surroundings. This side of the barn roof ends with a severe drop-off. On the other side, I might survive the fall from the edge of the roof. On this side, I'm not so sure. We had to replace the cedar shingles one time and I remember using Uncle Walt's longest ladder to do the top row, and securing the feet of the ladder on loose rocks below.

The good news is the shed. On my left, the barn attaches to the shed and that roof is probably only a five foot drop. It could be more. I try not to think about it too hard as I inch my way to the left. The pitch of the roof is steep. I have to keep most of my body in contact with the shingles or else I start to slide. I don't have a sense of how far down the roof I've already slid. Frankly, I don't want to know.

It's a simple process.

I reach out with my left hand and press my palm to the shingles. The day's heat is still radiating from the gray surface. Tiny pebbles roll away from my hand as I pretend that I have a grip. Lifting myself slightly, I try to slide my hips to the left without losing any height. I manage to arrest my fall after only slipping a couple of inches. Then, I slide my left foot over.

Meanwhile, I'm calculating. If I slip two inches for every inch of leftward progress, will I make it? Or will my foot soon slip over the edge, over open air. Once that happens, it's all over. Losing one toe of grip is going to doom me to a quick fall.

Uncle Walt would be horrified by all this. He and I installed some of these very shingles. Well, technically he installed them. I just cut the custom sizes he needed and handed them to him from the ladder. We built up the rows on the left side and then worked our way to the right, trying desperately to never put a foot down on a shingle once it was laid. According to him, every footstep took a month off of a shingle's life.

I manage to move three inches with my next effort.

I refuse to look up.

Yes, I hear that sound.

It's moving quite deliberately. I hear what must be fingernails or claws, gripping into the shingles as it climbs. The peak is the only safe place to traverse the roof. Up there, one can straddle both sides and make fast progress. That's where it must be headed.

I lay my face against the shingles as I attempt my next micro-shift to the left. Every tiny bit helps, I suppose.

In the past few years, I've been trying to learn to control my impulses. Patience was never my strongest quality. Putting together a jigsaw puzzle, I would find a piece that I was sure should fit. When it didn't, I would gather my fist and pound. That technique almost never leads to success.

I blame Fonzie.

There was this syndicated TV show when I was a kid. It was called *Happy Days*. The strongest, coolest character had the ability to punch his way to success. If he wanted the lights on, he would punch the wall. If he wanted to listen to music, punch the jukebox. With role models like that, it shouldn't be a surprise that I equate success with rash decisions.

I would like to make one now.

Creeping to the left is only prolonging my agony. I could simply slide down the roof, drop to the ground below, and hope for the best. What's the worst that could happen?

This is the kind of thinking that I'm trying to move away from.

(It seems like the sun should have come

up.)

It seems like the sun should have come up.

I feel like I've been creeping for hours and hours. Up at the peak of the roof, I can hear it tapping the shingles as it tracks my progress. I'm wondering if it's some kind of echolocation. Maybe it taps and knocks so it can hear the sound reflected off of me. I'm making a racket though—scraping my way across the shingles, trying not to slip. If it tracks by sound, I'm painting a picture with each inch that I move.

The tapping is unnerving, but at least I know where it is. I'm afraid to look.

I keep thinking about Mr. Engel. The heat is a perfect explanation for why he had collapsed on his kitchen floor and then later died. But what did Amber say? I believe it was something like aplastic anemia or a vitamin deficiency. Which was it? Did he fail to eat his vegetables, or was his blood thinned artificially?

Obviously, I can't help but focus on the sinister option. Whatever was down in his freezer—he deemed it a vampire— brought him to the brink of death. The heat simply pushed him over the edge. That's not exactly right though, is it? He didn't say that there was a vampire down in his cellar. He said *vampires*. Plural. That simple S on the end of the word is what I keep coming back to. I only saw one pair of eyes looking back at me when I opened the freezer and I was instantly entranced. What if there were other sets in there? The figure that I saw slip through the trapdoor of the barn's deck didn't look big enough to fill a freezer, that's for sure. At most, it was the slim shape of a young woman. How many more were in there?

My left hand finds a spot where the shingles are at a lower temperature. Going for broke, I reach farther and my hand finds the edge of the roof. I grip it tight. It's the first solid hold that I've had on anything since I tumbled from the railing. I exhale in relief.

The tapping stops.

I steal a glance upwards and I see a black silhouette start to maneuver away from the edge of the roof. It's returning to the right, back towards the deck. Am I being manipulated?

I look back down to the roof before the head can turn and it can catch me in its glare again.

I test my grip on the edge, pulling so I can climb up. The barn sticks out from the shed by, what, ten feet? How far do I have to ascend before I can swing over the edge and drop to the shed roof? I can't believe that I'm seriously considering that option. The shed roof isn't steep, but it's still going to be difficult to catch myself before I tumble. People fracture their skulls just falling out of a chair. How am I going to survive if I roll off the shed?

With my next pull, I slide a little more left. I manage to wedge the toe of my shoe on the edge of a shingle. With all apologies to Uncle Walt, I dig my foot in as I lean left. It takes a second before I can pick out the edge of the shed roof in the darkness. I'm higher than I expected.

The steeper angle of the barn roof means that I could close the distance if I slid back down towards the edge. That would also shrink my landing zone. I'll take my chances where I am.

I slide farther left, until my chest is halfway over.

I risk one more glance upward. I don't see it. While I've been repositioning myself, it has moved off of the peak. It might have gone back to the deck, or even back down through the hatch.

How smart is it? Did it coerce me into taking this path so I'll drop into its waiting arms below? Now that it's gone, perhaps I should consider climbing up to the peak.

"No," I whisper, shaking my head. Once I'm up at the top, getting away will be a slow process. I would rather get down to a flat surface again.

I swing my leg over.

The lip of the roof is cutting into me in unpleasant ways. I rotate my hips over and commit more of myself to the idea of dropping. Once the bulk of my body is over, there's no turning back. I'm going to slide down or over. They're both horrible ideas, but I've worked so hard for this. I have to take the plunge.

My hands claw at the shingles as I try to slow my inevitable fall. The shingles cut deeper into the scrape on my arm and then I'm falling again. I try to twist in the air.

In the darkness, I'm so disoriented that I have no idea what is happening. My foot hits something and I try to absorb the impact with my leg. Then, something crashes into my head or rather my head crashes into something. It must be the wall of the barn, but I don't know how I got spun around. My hand comes down weird and my wrist is bent backwards before I flip over and tumble. Then I'm falling again.

The scrape of the shingles is familiar.

I go over the edge head first. Dragging the toe of my left foot, helps me slow down and spin. When I hit the ground below, I land on my right shoulder. Something pops in my arm and I roll away from the pain. The dirt is softer than I imagined.

I blink up at the stars and I have one blessed second where I'm thrilled that I survived at all. Anything beyond this point is pure gravy. My next breath dulls my enthusiasm. A shooting pain stifles my inhalation. It feels like a knife has been shoved between my ribs.

That's when I think about Mr. Engel again. I remember the panic in his eyes as he lay on his kitchen floor. He knew that death was coming and he was not at peace with the idea. I shouldn't be either. I have to get up. I have to find safety.

Whatever was up on top of the barn tapping on the roof, it's not be alone.

I push myself up with my left hand, protecting my right arm instinctively. It takes me a second to catch my breath. Every time I try to take in air, my muscles tense up, anticipating the pain. It stabs me again and again.

Pushing up to my knees, my chest hurts a little less. My head is ringing.

I stumble to my feet and catch myself by leaning against the shed. From here, It's about the same distance around the house as around the barn. There are no doors on this side of the house. I think that the terrain is easier around the house so I start to move that direction. If I had a key for the front door, that would be the quickest path. I don't. As far as I know, there never has been a key for that door. I'll have to go all the way around to the side door.

I'm still leaning against the wall when I reach the transition between the shed and the house.

Assessment

(It's time to reassess.)

It's time to reassess.

I don't know much of anything about navigating a big city. I have tons of ideas, but very little real world experience. This isn't a non sequitur, I swear.

There are predators in any city—people who would like to take your money, possessions, or worse—but a lot of us are never going to run into them. Staying safe is a matter of both attitude and luck. We can move around on streets that are already well populated, and stay out of dark alleys, of course. Also, we can mind our own business and walk with unwavering purpose so we don't get distracted by attempts to draw our attention. There's also the matter of fear. I think that someone who is obviously anxious and wary might be a ripe target. They project their weakness and draw the predators to themselves.

So, by staying with the pack and maintaining the right mindset, we can reduce the odds that we'll be preyed upon.

But what happens if we're approached?

What do we do if someone steps in our path and initiates a conversation?

If you escalated immediately to panic, could you avoid

conflict? If someone makes eye contact, should you turn and bolt? It would be an inconvenient strategy. But I wonder—aren't victims most likely the ones who trade their safety for convenience? You cut across the park because it's the shortest way home and you walk right into a mugging.

I'm not going to make the mistake of underestimating the danger here.

I need to make rational decisions. I'm not going to let myself panic.

But I'm not going to just lie down on the kitchen floor like Mr. Engel.

My arm is scraped, my right shoulder feels like it's stiffening up, and my head hurts. My legs work just fine. When I have to fight, I'll do best to stick to my left arm. I can't look in its eyes—I have to remember that. They were too mesmerizing.

Something is moving around inside the house—I see a shadow move through the light spilling from the window and hear a tapping. I don't know how it got inside. I shouldn't be surprised. It found a way into the barn.

That leaves me with one option—the truck. I take out my keys and study them with my fingers until I find the one with the square top. That's the ignition key for the truck. The doors are unlocked. All I have to do is get around the house, jump inside the truck, and get the doors locked.

I duck below the light from the window and make my way along the side of the house.

It would be stupid to assume that there's only one of them. One might be exploring inside while another patrols the front.

I pause at the corner and angle my head around the side.

The bushes are blocking my view of the front porch. Uncle Walt used to cut them way back every spring. I think he missed the last few. They throw reaching shadows out into the yard.

I wait, looking for any movement.

The tapping coming from inside the house is back.

Was I right before? Is it some kind of echolocation? The eyes are captivating, but maybe they're just for show. Maybe it navigates only through sound. If that's true, its hearing could be really acute. I can't afford to make any noise.

Instead of dashing around the bush and sticking close to the house, I slip away at a diagonal until I'm beyond the pool of light from the windows. My feet brush through he tall grass at the edge of where I mow.

There's a shape crouching on the porch, under the bird feeder again. I look down and freeze, watching the shape in my peripheral vision. It looks like the head has snapped up. I hold my breath. I think it's sniffing the air, or maybe just turning its head, trying to listen for me.

I sneak a glance, immediately regretting it.

Even at this distance, I catch sight of the eyes. This one is different—the eyes seem to glow a little green. Squeezing my eyes shut, I manage to turn my head away.

I hear light tapping in the air. It sounds like a hard fingernail thumping against stone. To make sure they don't jingle, I'm gripping the keys so hard that they're digging into my palm. I can't get caught here, frozen by fear.

When I start moving again, the tapping stops.

My eyes are locked on the bush as I step, foot over foot along the edge of the tall grass. It's turning its head again, listening or sniffing.

The bush is just about to obscure my view of it, and then I'll reach the corner of the house. From there, it would be a quick sprint to the truck. If I lose sight of it, I won't know if it's staying on the porch. I won't know if I should continue to creep or just sprint.

This is that situation—I'm the rube in the city. If I assume that it's *not* creeping behind the bush, and along the side of the house, then I won't know until it springs out from behind the corner of the house. I have to assume the worst.

With no more delay, I sprint.

(I can't run fast enough.)

I can't run fast enough.

My legs are pumping beneath me, but the speed won't come. It's like I'm moving through molasses, or trying to run up a sand dune. A shadow shifts on my left and I whip my head to see that it's my own shadow. That was a stupid mistake. If I had seen more of those mesmerizing eyes, I would be caught. In slow motion, I turn my eyes back towards my goal. The truck looks like it's getting farther away with each sprinting stride.

The keys jangle and sing. I'm gripping only the ignition key. My shoulder throbs each time I pump that arm in time with my legs.

I reach out and put on the brakes too late. After crashing into the passenger's door, I claw it open and dive inside. My first attempt closes the door on my own shoe. I contract my leg and slam it home. With my elbow, I drive down the near lock. The keys go flying as I reach for the other one.

With both doors locked, I pull myself over the bench seat and slide the rear window closed so I can latch it.

Something has moved in front of the truck.

I submerge my head below the dashboard and reach around.

The keys have disappeared. The cab of the truck isn't that big. They have to be here somewhere.

I hold my breath when I hear something bump into the body of the truck.

I can't look up.

It's almost painful, but I squeeze my eyes shut while my hand searches for the key. My heartbeat echoes in my chest. My fingers map the terrain of the truck's floor mat.

When I was a kid, I sucked at running. Even two laps around the soccer field would make me want to throw up. Another boy in my class—Luke Mason, maybe?—taught me to take three strides for every time I take a breath. It doesn't always work. When I first start running I have to pant until my body

Ike Hamill

settles into the rhythm. I still try to use Luke's method. It makes me focus on my breathing until it comes under control. So that's what I do now—focus on my breath. My hand scans back and forth three times, making three passes at the floor, and I take a breath. Over the next three passes, I let it out.

Fingertips brush something metal. It moves.

Finally, I find the keys under the seat.

I fish them out slowly, fearing that if I ease my grip they'll disappear again.

They jingle together and I hear something tap on the door right next to my head.

Whatever is out there, it's only inches away from me now. Only metal and glass keep it at bay.

My eyes are still shut tight as I push up and squeeze between the steering wheel and the seat. I don't know how many of them are out there. I don't know if they're smart enough to find a rock and smash through one of the side windows.

When I'm sitting in the middle of the seat, face still scrunched up to keep my eyes shut, I pull on the steering wheel to slide into the driver's seat.

Even through my eyelids, it's like I can still see a pair of glowing eyes. Maybe the hypnosis isn't just visual.

My trembling hand guides the key into the side of the steering column. I pull back and try three more times until the key finds its slot.

The key turns and clicks.

The sound is echoed by a tap on the window.

What is that thing? It's shaped like a person, but it has to be some kind of cunning animal, right? It's a blind, glowing-eyed, hypnotizing predator that Mr. Engel described as a vampire.

I turn the key almost all the way to ignition when I remember the transmission. Uncle Walt taught me to always leave the truck in first gear when I park it. I stand on the clutch and pull the shifter out of gear before my hand finds its way back to the key.

The starter grinds and whines. It seems like an eternity

102

before the thing catches. I punch the accelerator and the engine roars under the hood, sending a throbbing vibration up through my feet.

Now what?

The dooryard is pretty big. I would normally back around to the left and then crank the wheel back to the right in order to turn out to the road. The tapping on my window is increasing in speed. It's getting ready to do something. How far can I drive using muscle memory before I have to open my eyes? There's a ditch that runs along the length of the field and passes under the driveway. Uncle Walt used to have sections of fence on either side, acting like a guard rail between the driveway and the ditch. It rotted away years ago and we never replaced it. The fence just made it difficult to mow the grass that would grow up around the ends the culvert.

Now, I can only pray that I don't need it.

I spin the steering wheel and push the shifter into reverse. It clunks home.

The speed of the tapping increases even more.

How many of them are there? Is there still one in front of the truck? Is it scurrying after me as the tires throw gravel and I back away?

I brought Kimberly up to Maine once. It was right after she found out that she was pregnant. We went to the fair out in Windsor, and I bought tickets and rode the twisting and spinning rides alone. Kimberly made fun of me every time I staggered down the metal stairs, trying to get my balance.

"Why are you torturing yourself like this?" she asked every time.

My answer never changed. "One day, maybe eight years from now, our child is going to drum up the courage to ride these and they're going to want me to ride with them. I'm just practicing for that day so I don't throw up."

The truth was that I liked the feeling. The rides made me nauseous, but I still liked the feeling of being thrown left, right, up, and down with zero control. The queasy stomach was a small price to pay. It's almost the same way now. Driving in a tight, fast arc with my eyes closed, my stomach flops and my head spins. I desperately want to open my eyes so I can lock onto some distant point and make sense of the way that I'm accelerating.

Tonight, the feeling of being out of control isn't welcome at all.

Ditch

(Time is relative.)

Time is relative.

I know that this isn't an original thought. It's not even particularly creative. I remember when it first occurred to me. I was standing in the kitchen, eating a piece of buttered bread. My mother was racing around, trying to make sure she had everything she needed before we left on our trip. Mom was a blur, racing from the hall, through the kitchen, and then disappearing into the living room while she stuffed a folder of papers into her bag.

Passing by me, she said something like, "I certainly hope you packed your toothbrush. There's not going to be a single store open when we get there."

I did have my toothbrush. Everything I needed for the week was stuffed into my backpack and that was planted firmly on the floor between my feet.

The next time I saw mom, she was headed the opposite direction with an armload of folded clothes.

"And who knows if the washing machine will be in working order. Last time I spent a fortune in quarters at the laundromat. I'm not doing that again."

I had enough underwear to last. I wasn't worried. Besides, I didn't plan on wearing anything besides a bathing suit. We were headed to the beach. For a few years, before she started shipping me off to Uncle Walt's for the summer, we stayed at the beach. Her "friend" had a place that he let us borrow. The first thing Mom would do when we arrived would be to gather up all the pictures of her "friend" and his wife and stuff them deep in a drawer in the dining room. At the end of the trip, Mom would return the pictures to where they belonged.

When she finally finished her preparations and stood by the front door, she turned back to me with a scowl.

"Are you coming, or are you going to make me wait all day?" she asked.

In her mind, the time packing and racing around was nothing. The few seconds she stood by the door, waiting for me to finish my bread, was a lifetime. Time is relative. I noticed it more and more after that moment. The trip to get to the beach took a century. The return home to my mundane life was over in a blink.

I wake up to the sound of the truck's horn. It sounds distant, almost sounding like a train horn in the fog. As I blink and push back from the steering wheel, it stops. I yawn and pop my ears.

The tapping starts almost immediately.

I nearly turn to look at the source, and then I remember.

It all comes flooding back.

I backed up fast, perhaps turning too far before I pushed the shifter into first. Then I must have overshot the driveway and crashed into the culvert. Without my seatbelt on, I had cracked my head against the hard plastic steering wheel and then slumped into the horn.

I can feel a lump rising on my forehead.

There's another tapping coming from the right side now.

At least two of them are tapping.

I put the shifter back in reverse, push the clutch, and start the engine again. It rolls back into life. The rear wheels pull the truck back a foot or two and then spin. Something is caught. The front wheel could be stuck on the culvert, or maybe the remnants of the old fence. I spin the steering wheel left and then right, trying to get free.

There's not enough traction to build up any momentum. When I press in the clutch, I feel the truck roll forward again. I try to rock it back and forth to spring loose. One time, my uncle used this technique to get the front tire over a rock when he got stuck behind the barn. It worked for him, but I can't seem to get the rhythm right.

The tapping is getting stronger and stronger.

Maybe they're not trying to echolocate me—maybe it's just an effort to draw my attention so I'll look into their hypnotic eyes. It almost works. I want to see what's making that sound. When I open my eyes, looking straight forward, I can see the glow in my peripheral vision. They're definitely on either side of the truck. There may be more than two.

I let the gearshift settle into neutral and I take my foot off the gas. I'm idling in the ditch.

The tapping matches the speed of my thudding heart.

I take a breath and try to hold it, imagining myself running three strides before I let it out.

An image takes shape in my head. It's Mr. Engel's house. There are two trees flanking the building and two windows on either side of the front door. On the second floor, I see three windows across the face. One of those windows belongs to Mr. Engel's bedroom. I've been up there. The third floor has just the one window and it's smaller than the others—four panes over four panes.

Four by four.

Four...

"Wheel drive," I whisper. My eyes fly open and I fumble for the switch on the dashboard that controls the lights. When they come on, I focus on the green glow of the radio and then carefully study the knobs and switches below that.

It's not a switch I'm looking for though. If the truck were

more recent, maybe it would be, but I'm looking for the second shift lever—the one I've ignored all these years. I never drove up here in the winter time, so I never had cause to touch it. I guess that over time my eyes grew accustomed to skipping right over it.

It's pushed all the way forward into two-wheel drive. I push the clutch and clunk it back into four high.

This time when I close my eyes, I'm praying that four-wheel drive will get me out of the ditch. I put the truck into reverse and ease into the gas.

The front hangs up again and the back wheel spins.

The answer pops into my head immediately.

I haven't switched the hubs yet. Uncle Walt had to get out and engage the locking hubs on the front wheels before four-wheel drive would work. I had a really good look at those the other day when I was changing the flat.

I bang my head back against the headrest and let out a disgusted sigh.

Listening to the engine idle, something occurs to me—there's no tapping.

When did they stop?

I have an idea.

I reach forward and shut off the lights, holding my breath and waiting.

Before I hear it, my lungs are burning and I have to breathe again.

By my best guess, it takes almost a thirty seconds for the tapping to return. But, like I said, time is relative. Is that enough time for me to engage the locking hubs? What if I just do the one on the left side? What if the lights don't actually drive them away? What if my conjecture is completely wrong?

When I turn on the lights again, the tapping stops immediately. I count to thirty anyway.

My hand finds the lock and I gather my courage.

There's no other way, right? I have to get out of here and getting the four-wheel drive engaged is my only hope.

The image of Mr. Engel's house appears in my head again. It's a perfect New England house, flanked by perfect trees. It could be on a jigsaw puzzle—that's how perfect it is. I don't know why someone chose to build it in the middle of nowhere. The house would be right at home in the center of town, on Main Street.

In my imagination, the sun is directly overhead. This time of year, the front of the house would face the rising sun at...

"Dawn," I whisper.

What was I thinking? I don't have to blunder out into the night and try to lock the hub. They haven't shown any ability to break the windows and the headlights seem to keep them at bay. Why would I risk leaving the truck when it's possible that all I have to do is wait until dawn?

I lean forward and cup my hands around my eyes so I can confirm something.

Yes—the tank is nearly three-quarters full. I'm guessing that the truck could idle all night with the lights on. Then, when the sun rises, they'll go away to hide in a basement somewhere. I'll be able to waltz outside and take my time locking the hubs and extracting the truck from the ditch. Hell, I could probably stroll inside and use the phone.

"No," I whisper, shaking my head.

That's right—the phone is dead. I have to keep my wits. Let's not forget the hard lessons I've learned.

I settle into the seat and try to relax. I might need my strength.

(The waiting is the hardest part.)

The waiting is the hardest part.

I have the radio on very low. Every few seconds, I turn it all the way down so I can listen for sounds of movement outside the truck. Then, I turn it back up. Focusing on the lyrics is the only way that I'm staying awake, and I desperately want to stay awake. In the middle of the night, eyes closed, windows up, with the gentle vibration of the engine, staying awake is a nearly impossible task.

Tom Petty reminds me one last time that the waiting is the hardest part and then he's on to another tale. Now he's telling me that I wreck him. I don't think he's talking to me.

When I was a kid, my mom really liked to listen to Anne Murray. Mom had a scratched up record from the seventies that she would put on when she took a bath. In South Carolina, the stereo was in the living room and it was my job to flip the album while she soaked. Through the slightly-open door, I would hear the occasional slosh of water and see the flickering candlelight.

I never understood the lyrics. Some of the songs seemed to talk about empowerment, but always with the backdrop of a supporting man. A woman could stand on her own as long as the ground was stabilized by a good, strong, man first. I never thought of my mom as weak. If she could have seen herself the way that I saw her, I'm sure she would have understood that a weak person couldn't have done the things that she did.

Maybe Anne Murray was the same way.

I guess I inherited some of Mom's learned helplessness. I learned to ride my bike by pushing off with my feet and then holding them to the sides while I coasted around. I would only rest my feet on the pedals when my legs got too tired. I didn't realize that I was already doing all the hard parts of riding a bike —balancing and steering. Still convinced that I didn't really know how to ride, I would stay home when the other kids rode to the store or down to the creek.

The girl next door, Shelby, chastised me one day.

She said, "You think you're too good to ride bikes with us. You're stuck up."

I blushed, looked down, and scuffed my foot on the pavement. I really liked Shelby. I finally admitted to her that I didn't know how to ride.

"Yes you do, liar. I see you ride all the time on the dirt road behind the apartments."

I explained that all I could do was coast.

"Pedaling is the easy part. You just push down."

She showed me in about three seconds. The first time I tried, I pushed down with both feet at the same time and lifted myself off the seat. When I fell over, Shelby laughed at me and my scraped arm.

"One at a time, dummy."

The second time was like magic. Pedaling was almost easier than coasting. Something about the extra torque stabilized the bike even more. Shelby and I were riding down to the store a few minutes later and I rode so fast that I thought I might take flight.

I had taught myself the hardest parts and it was only my lack of confidence that had stood in my way. Shelby hadn't really helped me, she had just pointed out that I didn't need anyone's help. I wonder if Mom ever came to that same realization. If she did, she never told me. Until she died, she still seemed to be looking for someone to take care of her. She wanted someone to make sure the ground was firm so that she could stand up straight and proud.

They would never play Anne Murray on the Mountain of Pure Rock.

I turn the radio down again and listen to the idling engine.

When I turn it back up, it's Pink Floyd. Airy and smooth melodies are not what I need right now.

I hear a tapping on the roof of the truck and I snap off the radio and hold my breath. With my hands cupped over my eyes, I sneak a peek directly forward to verify that the headlights are still on. The tapping isn't as consistent as before. It sounds like random plunks against the metal.

A second later, I realize why.

"Rain," I whisper, chancing another peek. Sure enough, there are drops on the windshield.

I should have guessed. After all, that's why I had made sure to put the truck windows up before I went to bed. There had been the chance of rain.

I wonder if they're still out there in the rain. I wonder if they're getting wet, waiting just beyond the circle of light cast by my headlights.

I turn up the radio a little and the DJ tells me that we have Bad Company, Candlebox, and Soundgarden coming up after the break. He doesn't mention the time. I wonder if his voice is prerecorded. The clock on the dash is stuck at three.

I have no idea how many hours are left until dawn.

Just for something to do, I grope around on the radio until I find the tuning knob. Making a slow sweep, I go from one end to the other. Buried in static, I find a voice but I can't really make out what he's saying. It must be religious. The only word that I catch is "Temptation." I wander back to the Mountain and listen to an ad for a car dealership and then a furniture store.

The rain slows down.

(I remember the phone.)

I remember the phone.

I have to keep my wits. The cordless phone was working, but the line was dead. Since moving to my uncle's place, I've never had issues with the internet service or the phone. It would be stupid to assume that it's a coincidence that the phone outage and my visitors were unrelated. Therefore, it would be stupid to assume that they're simply cunning animals. They must be intelligent enough to understand that the phone is connected by the cable and that they could cut me off from the outside world by severing that line. If they're smart enough to do that, what else are they smart enough to figure out?

One of my favorite movies had a great line: "What do you mean, 'they cut the power'? How could *they* cut the power, man? They're animals."

Because they didn't smash the window of the truck, I've been assuming that they're not too bright. What if there's another reason?

Maybe they don't like to break glass. Maybe the sound hurts their ears the same way that the light hurts their eyes.

"Pieces," I whisper.

I'm thinking about the one on the front porch and how it was crouched under the bird feeder. Didn't I read somewhere that a vampires are compelled to count spilled seeds? I think that's the way it goes. People used to put a pile of seeds on their porch because a vampire would be compelled to count them before passing.

Maybe it's the same with shards of glass?

This is all speculation. At least it's occupying my brain and helping me stay awake.

Suffice to say, there could be a logical reason that they haven't smashed my window besides simple stupidity. If that's true, I'm going to have to stay on my toes.

I take a peek at the dash.

The clock is still dead at three. The gas is holding out—more than half a tank.

The Mountain of Pure Rock, WTOS, is fulfilling their promise of Soundgarden. I don't recognize the song, but Chris Cornell's voice is unmistakable. I wonder how many voices I've heard tonight are from dead people. Petty is dead. Cornell is dead. I'm pretty sure that the guy from Bad Company—Paul Rodgers?—is still alive. I wonder if there's a correlation between how long a musician is remembered and the tragic circumstances of their death. If they just pass away from natural causes, does their music fade away fast? At the moment, I can't think of any dead musicians who didn't die in a horrific way.

Mr. Engel didn't die in a horrific way, at least not according to the hospital. They said it was a kind of anemia. I wonder if that's what they will say about me. Will two cases of anemia be enough to trigger suspicion. I hate the idea that there's a chance that they will kill me too and nobody will put two and two together.

That's one thing that I have control over.

I reach past the shifter and feel across the dash until I find the glove compartment. Inside, there's a notepad with a pencil through the spiral binding. For a long time, Uncle Walt wrote down the miles and gallons every time he filled the truck. He said that a sudden change in gas mileage was a good indicator that there was a problem brewing with the truck. I guess he gave up on the idea at some point because the last time I looked the notebook didn't have any recent entries.

It was about to get one. I crawl over to the passenger's side and lower myself into the footwell.

When I'm crouched low, I open my eyes.

I can just see the notebook from the light of the dashboard.

I flip to a blank page and start writing.

I mention Mr. Engel and how I found him. The word "vampire" only appears in my narrative as a quote from Mr. Engel. I don't want anyone to assume that I'm crazy. I only refer to them as predatory animals. It's a simplification, but I'm trying to maintain the credibility of the narrative. I beseech anyone who finds my body to look into the possibility that I was a victim of these animals. I reiterate that I have no history of anemia. I donate blood all the time with no issues.

My handwriting has deteriorated in the past couple of years.

Kimberly and I used to leave notes for each other all the time. We had a certain style in these notes that's hard to describe. You might call it Victorian Nonsensical Love Letter style. She started it, of course. I came home one day and found a note that said something like:

Dearest, I pray this missive finds you well. The furry one— firm decision being unnatural to his bearing—is neither in nor out. He stood in the doorway mewling whilst I prepared my lunch and I fear I've lost track of him. Henceforth, I shall call him Schrödinger and wonder everlasting over his existence. On the morrow, we're expected in Danforth. Until tonight, my heart beats for both of us.

My replies were never as clever as hers, but I tried. With all that writing, my hand grew confident and the script was confident and legible. I've lost that skill apparently. I read over my note and make a few clarifying smudges where necessary.

When she was pregnant, her body bulging and stretching, she trusted her doctor completely. Dr. Phan had four kids of her own and she was very honest about the experience of her own pregnancies. Dr. Phan would say, "You're unlikely to experience anything more painful than your first birth, but don't worry, you're unlikely to remember it accurately."

Kimberly had laughed at that. Her memory was great. She took pride in it.

Dr. Phan said, "It's self defense, really. If women were honest with themselves over the pain, the human race would be extinct in a generation."

I was horrified by the idea and I wished that Dr. Phan would stop trying to frighten Kimberly. But Kimberly wasn't scared by the warnings. She seemed glad that someone was being forthcoming and not trying to sugarcoat the upcoming trauma.

I suppose that it's the same way with any kind of pain. Our ability to feel is way more honed than our ability to remember. The best and the worst things in our lives are dulled when we try to imagine them. I hate that. I want to remember precisely the crushing weight of loss. To forget the pain of losing Kimberly and our baby is an insult to their monumental importance. The fact that I continue to breathe and my heart continues to beat is unthinkable. My entire world ended that day and yet my stubborn body continues to live. These sentiments would fit well in a Victorian Nonsensical Love Letter.

I close the notebook and reach up to put it on the dashboard. After a moment of reflection, I move it to the glove compartment.

I settle back down into the footwell. My legs are threaded between the shift levers and I lean back against the passenger's door. Down here, it feels safe to open my eyes and stare down at my hands.

The Mountain of Pure Rock is playing a block of Heart. Ann Wilson sings like she's trying to be Robert Plant and then plays the flute like she's Ian Anderson. I wonder if Heart should be considered innovative because they were women who could match the best of the male rockers, or if they were simply derivative of the most popular trends of their time. I've been listening to this station for too long.

(I've fallen into the well.)

I've fallen into the well.

My memories of Kimberly are a well. There are no rocks at the bottom. It's only quicksand. Even if I drown, I'll never stop sinking into them.

Before her, I used to think that there were two types of people—pleasant people and interesting people. The ones I found pleasant were always operating on the surface. They were polite and upbeat, but not willing to open up to anything deeper. The interesting people were almost always a little bitter or unpleasant. I probably fall into that category. I try to be optimistic, but every time I allow myself to focus on the positive, something knocks me upside the head and forces me to see the bad side of things.

Kimberly had layers.

We met at a picnic. Her neighbors invited her over. I came with a friend from work. The three of us fell into a debate over potato chips. Right away, I could tell that she wasn't interesting. She maintained the position that Ruffles were just as good as kettle cooked chips, while I argued the opposite.

"They taste just as good, but you can eat more of them without hurting your mouth," she said.

"Hurting your... Are you twelve?" my friend asked. "Just chew the chips instead of mashing them into your cheeks and gums."

I waved him off. He was being way too aggressive for a casual picnic conversation.

"Forget the texture," I said. "I don't think you've properly considered the question of taste. Try these two, side by side, and tell me that the taste of your Ruffles is just as good."

She raised her eyebrows and tried both. In deference to my friend's point, she carefully crunched the chips between her teeth as she chewed.

"I suppose you have a point," she said when she was done.

That's when I thought the conversation was over. An interesting person would have found a way to continue the debate and get a few more laughs out of the conversation. Kimberly was too pleasant to be deep, or so I incorrectly concluded.

Honestly, I didn't even consider her beautiful that first time we met.

Kimberly had layers.

The next time I saw her, she was standing in line at the bagel shop next to the dealership where my car was being worked on. It had been a couple of months, so it took me a few minutes to remember where I had met her. I didn't come up with a name. When she turned and walked towards me, I pointed and said, "Ruffles!"

Immediately, she smiled and said, "Kettle chips."

"I'm waiting for my car," I said, gesturing through the window that faced the dealership.

"Join me," she said. "I'm on my lunch break."

I nodded and she turned to find a table in the corner.

Honestly, I was half annoyed as the line moved forward and I ordered a sandwich. It was presumptuous of her to assume that I would entertain her over her lunch just because I was waiting. Sometimes nice people do that—they make plans for you assuming that you're a nice person too. What if I had just wanted to be alone? I had half a mind to make an excuse about how I wanted to be over at the dealership when my car was finished. By the time I got my sandwich and paid, she was looking down at a book, oblivious to me. I could have walked right by.

"You must work for the insurance company," I said as I sat down. Aside from the dealership and the bagel place, it was the only business around.

She nodded and used her finger to wipe a dab of cream cheese from the corner of her mouth. I don't know what it was about that gesture. That was the first moment that I felt any attraction to her.

"I do," she said when she finished chewing. "You?"

We went through the normal details—work, apartments, brief history, etc.

Then, we reached layer two.

Kimberly had layers.

"Do you think life is short or long?" she asked.

"Life is short. Suffering is long," I said. "Why do you ask?"

She tapped the book as she shut it.

"I used to think of books as little miniature lives that I could live for the price of a number of hours," she said. "When I was a kid, I would dive into each new one and imagine that it had a particular lesson to impart to me, regardless of whether or not the author intended it. Dreams are simple rehashing of the day's events, giving us a chance to regard them with a fresh perspective. But books are so much more powerful. They're the rehashing of someone else's experience. That's a rare gift."

I've never been that into reading. I said as much. Narrative storytelling has moved on. We have movies now—literally and figuratively, they can show us so much more.

"So you're a 'life is short' person."

"Life is short. Suffering is long. Is this what you do on your lunch break? You contemplate the meaning of life?"

She smiled.

"Not the meaning. Just the duration. This book is long. Maybe it's too long—I can't tell yet."

I nodded.

We ate in silence for a little while. I tried to think of something deep to say. I wasn't trying to impress her. I just thought that she would appreciate something deep. My friends at work hated anything philosophical. It's not that they were anti-intellectual, it's just that... Actually, I suppose they were anti-intellectual. There was this whole thing with our pompous boss and it had... It's not important to the story.

"What do you think now?" I asked.

"Sorry?"

"You said that you used to think books were mini lives when you were a kid. What do you think of them now?"

She raised her eyebrows and took a sip of her drink before she answered.

"I think that very few books are intentionally about anything. That's not to say that they're empty of meaning. People sit down to write a book that's interesting to them. When they're done, maybe they go back and strengthen the obvious congruencies into a coherent theme. Maybe they just punch up the plot so that it moves well."

"So why are you still reading? Why haven't you given up on books?"

"What's interesting to the author is also interesting to me a lot of times. It makes me think. When I'm done, I've learned something just by the process. Whether the lesson was preconceived or not, a book still has something to teach."

"That could apply to any art," I said. "Why books?"

She picked the book up and waved it. "Portable."

We laughed.

Kimberly had layers.

It wasn't that she knew a lot of stuff—she did, but it wasn't about that. It was that she was curious and always trying to learn new things. I had become pretty cynical and mistrustful of the world by then. Pessimism works because it's almost always correct. You're not going to win the lottery. Studying hard is not going to make you ace the exam. Staying away from cigarettes doesn't mean that you won't die of lung cancer.

Optimism takes too much strength. You have to learn to live with being wrong most of the time.

Kimberly was strong, curious, and thoughtful.

She was also really interesting.

That's the part that I didn't expect.

Every day we were together, I felt myself becoming more and more optimistic. Every bad thing that had ever happened was fine. It all served to help me understand how blessed I was to be with her. Even the bad days we had together were just the shadows that helped the highlights sparkle even brighter.

When she died, I finally understood what had really been happening. I wasn't learning to be an optimist, I was poisoning her with my negativity. Light can't last forever. Darkness always wins.

I pledged the opposite the last time I held her hand. She had no idea what I was saying, I'm sure. I told her that I was going to raise our child to be happy and positive all the time. I was never going to let our child go to sleep upset. Every morning the sun would shine new light into their life. This was before I found out that our child was dead as well. Things took somewhat of a sour swing at that point, as you might imagine. I had no more promises to give and nobody to protect.

Coming

(It's three o'clock.)

It's three o'clock.

The woman on the Mountain of Pure Rock tells me so. I think that her shift has just begun. She sounds both chipper and weary, if that's a thing. We're about to kick things off with some Judas Priest and Black Sabbath to ring in the witching hour. Underneath her voice and the background music that accompanies her, I hear a scratching sound. When I reach up and turn down the radio, I realize that the scratching sound is coming from beneath me.

The truck lights are still on. I can see that the knob is pulled out.

I awkwardly roll over so I can press my ear against the rubber mat.

It's a rhythmic grinding sound that vibrates in the metal.

A horrible image pops into my head. Something approached through the weeds that have grown up in the opposite side of the culvert. Slowly, it squeezed into the tube of metal and pulled itself under the driveway, arching its back to stay above the stagnant water collected in the corrugated bottom. It emerged under the truck, safe from the light.

And now it's sabotaging something under the...

"Fuel line," I whisper.

I squeeze my eyes shut and extract myself from the footwell.

Sitting upright in the driver's seat feels unnatural now.

I lean forward and cup my hands around my face as I lean towards the dash. When I open my eyes, I blink at the green gauges until I can read them.

The gas is below half and I can actually see it falling. Once the engine stalls, how long will the lights stay on? The battery has always had enough juice to start the truck, but the starter does seem to slow down if it takes more than a few seconds to catch. I remember talking to Uncle Walt on the phone one time. He was angry because he had left the door slightly ajar and the truck's battery had been killed by the interior lights. How long had that taken? Had he replaced the battery since? I might have an hour or two of headlights—probably less.

"Then what?" I whisper.

Even without lights, they didn't do anything more than tap on the windows. Maybe it doesn't matter. Maybe the lights will go out, they will approach, tap, and I'll just ignore it until dawn. I could tie my shirt around my eyes so that even if I accidentally open them, it won't matter.

"Smarter," I whisper.

Right—or maybe they're getting smarter.

Anything that could figure out how to cut a gas line could surely figure out how to get into the truck, right? If they're getting smarter and they're this determined, I'm in trouble.

Makes me wonder why they're this determined.

I took away Mr. Engel. I flushed them from their hiding place. I brought the police into the matter. It could be that they're just starving and I'm the only food source around.

The gas gauge is now descending towards a quarter of a tank. I imagine that the fuel is spilling out into the ditch and flowing into the culvert.

Mr. Engel said that they don't like heat.

From my experience, they don't like light.
I can extrapolate that they *really* don't enjoy...
"Fire."

PART FOUR:

REDEMPTION

Explosion

(Any doubt is gone.)

Any doubt is gone.

When I roll down the window an inch, the smell of gasoline greets me. This is a really stupid idea. It's also a really compelling idea. There's a whole, "Blaze of Glory," theme to it that I might have picked up from the Mountain of Pure Rock. We had a Bon Jovi block a few minutes ago.

After tearing out a few of the pages, I stuff the notebook into my back pocket.

In my lap, I have the box of matches. I stuck a bunch of matchsticks between the box and lid, lined up like little soldiers.

I open my eyes.

None of this is going to work unless I can see. With the lights on, I'm pretty sure that none of them are close enough to mesmerize me with their eyes, but who knows. There's nothing to lose at this point.

I see the truck around me and the patch of grass that the headlights illuminate. In the rearview mirror, the red lights show me the general shapes of the dooryard. There are dark forms moving around in that space. I don't see them precisely, but I see the moving shadows.

I shut off the truck's engine and click off the radio. I push the keys into my pocket.

All I hear is the summer crickets and dripping fluid. That would be the last of the gasoline. The truck wasn't going to run much longer anyway.

With the engine off, the light from the headlights is already looking a little yellow. I put the truck into R so the reverse lights come on. The shadows behind me evaporate, parting to the sides away from the new glow.

I roll down the window the rest of the way.

When I shift my weight, I hear the one below the truck. Maybe it's moving to try to get a look at what I'm doing.

I pull myself through the window and onto the roof, leading the way with the box of matches. I have to work quickly and pray that everything goes perfectly. I have no right to hope. The scheme is outlandishly stupid.

Kneeling on the roof of my uncle's truck, I ball up the paper and use it to prop the box of matches at an angle, right near the edge of the roof. When the paper burns away, I want the box to fall through the flames, catch one or more of the matches, and allow the whole burning box to plunge down into the fuel-soaked ditch.

My hands are shaking.

I focus completely on the task in front of my hands. It's almost impossible to see in the ambient light of the headlights. The drifting shadows suggest that there might be several of them out there. It's hard to tell from my peripheral vision.

The box is balanced precariously.

I've forgotten to save aside a match.

With trembling fingers I try to delicately pluck one of the soldiers from the seam of the box and I nearly topple the entire structure. That would have been an epic fail. Losing everything but a single match would doom me. Somehow, everything wobbles and then stays in place.

I take a deep breath—the duration of three imaginary strides—and let it out slowly.

I strike the match against the truck and it hisses to life. The glow reveals the mark I've just made on the paint. My uncle was so proud of the paint job on this truck. Even while the frame rusted away, he had washed and waxed the body. The match had made a big white mark. I am about to do much worse.

I hold the dancing flame to the piece of paper until it catches.

The flames grow immediately and I hurry away, nearly falling into the truck bed.

I watch the burning paper as I back across the truck bed and reach into my pocket. Folding the notebook in half, I hurl it as far as I can. I want it to be away from me and the truck. It lands in the darkness just as the box begins to tip. The soldier matches catch too early. They're going to burn out before...

The box falls over the side of the truck.

I'm not ready.

In my silly plans, I should have already jumped down and started to run by now, but I'm frozen. I'm still convinced that nothing will happen.

Sparks jump from the box as it lands on the frame of the open window and balances there.

It's not going to work. If the box falls into cab, nothing will happen.

This is my only chance. I have to take it.

(Failure was inevitable.)

Failure was inevitable.

My body is moving in slow motion as I plant my hands and jump over the tailgate to fall into darkness. By the time I hit stones and dirt, everything is moving at regular speed again.

I still hear the crickets, the dripping fuel, and the light crackle of the burning box of matches, precariously balanced on the window frame of the driver's door.

I push off from the truck and my feet crunch once, twice, and three times before I breathe.

That's when the world ends.

I'm not far enough away. The light reaches me before the sound. It's a flash of brilliance, plastering my enormous shadow on the side of the house, and then I hear the whoomph. The shockwave hits me an instant later and I'm deaf before my feet leave the packed dirt.

My body flips in the air.

The truck is lifted by the explosion. A jet of flame shoots out from the end of the culvert. There's a shape under there.

I smash and skid across the dooryard. The shape under the truck emits a horrible screaming squeal. It sounds like rusty metal grinding, fingers on a chalkboard, and the frantic whine of a dentist's drill all at the same time. Burning, it pulls itself through the ditch as the truck rocks and settles back to rest.

I can't look away. I want to, but I'm not in control of my body yet.

I hear a pop and it stops screaming and stops moving. It's still burning as it freezes. It doesn't have a human shape at all anymore.

I see a shadow streak at the edge of the firelight.

I have to get up.

My ears were stuffed with cotton a moment ago. Now they're filled with a constant, high-pitched tone. It's lucky that my hearing was deadened by the explosion. I think if I had heard the scream unmuffled, it would have driven me crazy.

I push up slowly, trying to get my balance as I rise to my knees.

My shadow is still huge against the side of the house, but it's fading as the fire quickly dies. I stagger into a run. It seems like falling off the shed happened a million years ago, but my shoulder remembers quite well. The pain flares when I try to get the keys out of my pocket. I force my fingers to work and transfer the keys to the other hand as I fall into the door.

There's another flash and blast from behind me. This

explosion sends shrapnel raining down. I unlock the door and push inside just as a chunk hits the house beside me.

I press the door shut behind me and lock it.

My hearing is returning to normal. I hear a deep groan and I shuffle to my right through broken glass. Peering through the shattered panes, it takes me a moment to figure out the source of the sound. The telephone pole is creaking and swaying. Near the base, part of it is burning and a chunk is missing. The cables have picked up a swing and they're wrenching the pole in two.

It lets out an enormous snap when it goes. I back up a pace as it falls. The pole slams down into the top of the burning truck. Sparks fly when the transformer smashes into the ground. The lights in the house dim, surge, and then extinguish. The kitchen is lit only by the dancing glow of the flames.

Out in the night, I hear another screech. This one doesn't sound like a cry of pain. This sounds like a war cry. A chill runs down my back.

From the living room, I hear tapping.

They're tapping on the glass and the walls. They won't come in through the kitchen—I'm almost certain of that. I have an idea that the broken glass will discourage them. It won't *stop* them, but it will discourage them. I have to retreat to the pantry. I've re-weighed my options that one is no longer as heavy on my heart as it was before. I'm forgetting something, but I'll have time to think when I get to...

The door won't open.

It takes me a moment.

I can't believe it.

I wedged the door shut with a broom before I fled. It seemed like such a reasonable idea at the time.

With my jaw hanging, I turn. The truck fire is already burning down. The light coming through the broken window used to be yellow. Now it's orange. Soon it will be little more than a campfire. How much can they endure?

I have to move fast.

(How long has it been?)

How long has it been?

Uncle Walt used to call it David's door. I never found out why. It's a black door in the side of the shed and it probably went unlocked for decades before I turned the mechanism a few hours ago. I locked it from the inside. I never checked the outside to make sure that the keyway wasn't jammed with dirt or rust or whatever. So, of course it is.

The smell of the burning truck is terrible. It scorches my nose and lungs.

I try to quietly work the key into the slot. The other keys are jingling with each movement. I can hear them tapping on the other side of the building, away from the firelight.

The key is halfway in and stuck.

I have no other options.

The truck fire will be gone before long. The power line is down. I had to jump over the dead wire just to get to David's door.

Something is moving under the shed.

On the other side of the building, the crawlspace is open. On my side, there's a loose stone foundation. Uncle Walt was planning on sealing up the whole space to keep the porcupines out, but he never got it finished.

In the dancing light, I see a slender finger emerge from between two rocks. Its long fingernail taps on the stone and then points to me. I'm frozen in fear as the process repeats.

I force myself to return my attention to the key. I'm on my tiptoes as I jerk the key loose and then shove it back in with enough force to bend metal.

The finger taps three times and then points. Could they somehow hear with their fingers? Is that even possible?

Another finger joins the first. They tap in a galloping cadence and pause.

I'm holding my breath and I've nearly forgotten about the key. The fingers are enduring the light from the truck fire. It's not bright enough to keep me safe.

I twist the key hard enough to break it.

Somehow, I get lucky and the cylinder turns. The door swings inward.

I remember when I was chased across the roof. I had the distinct feeling that I was being herded towards the edge. What if that's true now? What if the fingers are driving me inside towards something else that lurks in the darkness of the shed? There are no windows in this part.

Another long finger has emerged from a gap between different rocks. How many of them are down there?

That settles it—slip inside the shed and shut the door behind me, locking it again with the handle.

I've left the keys dangling from the outside knob. I'll need those to get into the pantry. When I open the door again, the burning truck in the distance looks like safety compared to the dark shed. It's difficult not to run across the dooryard and huddle by that fire. This must be how my ancestors survived predators, way back when. The allure is strong, but I ignore it. When I jerk the keys from the knob, I slam David's door shut again.

There's a tiny light down at the far end of the shed.

It has to be something battery operated, since the power is out. I don't have anything electric down there though. The tractor is down that way, but it's too old to have...

When the light shifts, I see that it's actually two lights. They're spaced apart the distance of eyes.

I turn and run for the pantry.

(In the darkness, they key finds the lock.)

In the darkness, the key finds the lock.

It's pitch black and my hand finds the doorknob as my other hand drives the key in.

I couldn't repeat that lucky move again if my life depended on it. I can hear something moving behind me as the key slips in, I turn the mechanism, and shove my way into the pantry. Ripping the keys out, I barely get my hand back through the gap before my body has slammed shut the door. It meets resistance before it latches. There's something on the other side of the door, scratching its way down until it finds the knob. I'm trying to turn the latch as it's trying to turn the knob. I can't engage the lock until I get the knob spun back around.

It's a battle that takes seconds. It feels like an epic struggle.

When the lock clicks and the knob freezes, I press my shoulder against the door to make sure it's really shut. Pain shoots down my arm and throbs in my shoulder. Adrenaline keeps making me forget about the injury. Each time the pain comes back, it's worse.

On the other side of the door, the scratching ends and tapping begins.

The shed felt like complete darkness. This is so much darker. I almost want to reach up and touch my face because it seems like there must be something covering my eyes.

The tapping descends.

It's moving around the door, tracing the perimeter.

I move forward and to my right with my hands extended until I find the kitchen door and the broom that's wedged in to keep it shut. I'm terrified that I might kick it loose and not be able to block the door again in the darkness.

What else is in here? I picture the pantry, taking a mental inventory of the space.

There's a small stepladder against the opposite wall, hung on a hook. When I was a kid, Uncle Walt could reach most of the lightbulbs just by elevating to his toes. Towards the end of his life, he became hunched over and had to use a ladder to even get to stuff on the top shelf. Mom sometimes teased him about his posture.

I fumble my way over to the ladder and lift it from the hook. Careful not to disturb the broom, I discover that the ladder will fit on the floor between the door and the far wall with only an inch to spare. The door normally swings inward—if the broom breaks, the ladder will act as a stop.

With that done, I settle to the floor, press my back against the door to the shed, and drape my legs over the ladder. The tapping slows and then stops.

My eyes are open so wide that they sting. I force myself to blink and then I see a tiny glimmer. There's a trace of orange light visible under the door to the kitchen. That's the last of the truck fire burning down. That little crack beneath the door is my connection to the outside world. If morning ever comes, that's how I'll know. The kitchen gets the sunrise first.

I reach up to the shelf and feel around until I find a box of graham crackers. Uncle Walt used to have them on hand for his "sweet tooth." When I was a kid, I thought they tasted like eating the cardboard of an old shoe box.

Uncle Walt would say, "The taste buds of an adult are less sensitive because they're tempered by a million disappointments."

He passed along a lot of wisdom over the years. He never once addressed what to do if I was trapped in the pantry by an unknown number of ravenous vampires.

I smile to myself in the dark.

Dark

(Sleep would be awesome.)

Sleep would be awesome.

It's out of the question though. I have to pee so bad that my bladder throbs with every heartbeat. I've been over my mental inventory of this place a dozen times and I can't think of anything that I could pee into. There's a big jar of pickles on one of the shelves, but then what will I do with the pickles?

Here's my plan so far: fish the pickles out of the jar, put the pickles into the empty graham cracker box, drink the pickle juice, and then pee into the pickle jar.

It's a terrible plan.

When I started first grade, I didn't know a single other kid in the school. Mom had picked us up and moved us in the middle of August. I spent weeks sitting on curbs while she went around and tried to find a job. Then one day she took me to a big brick building and announced that I would be going to school there. It was horrible.

I had been to school before, of course. My preschool was at a nice church, and my kindergarten had been at this really pretty old farmhouse in the country. We had learned the alphabet out in the garden. Math was taught in the kitchen.

In comparison, my new school looked like a prison.

Mom dropped me off and then strode away fast, swinging her purse and turning the corner before I could even start to cry. The kids all shunned me and my puffy face. Who could blame them? We had a small break after lunch and before we had to sit down for our next lesson. I was at the water fountain when one kid finally approached. I thought he wanted to be my friend.

He asked, "What's the right word for pee?"

"Huh?"

"What do you say when you mean pee?"

"Huh?"

"The real word."

I looked up and down the hall, trying to figure out what to do. All I could think was that this was a new way to make fun of me. This kid had grown tired of making fun of my snotty nose and decided that he would ask me nonsense questions until I went crazy.

"What?" I asked.

"Urinate?"

"That's a word," I said.

"So I say there's urinate on the floor?"

I finally figured out what he meant. My mom was big into the proper names of things, or I never would have been able to come up with the answer.

"Urine," I said. "You say that there's urine on the floor."

"Right," he said. He walked away.

I overheard him talking to the teacher when I went back to my seat. He said, "Someone had an accident in the bathroom. There's urine all over the floor."

Mrs. Baker said, "Thank you, Ted. That's a very polite way to tell me that."

I wanted to take credit. Ted was getting praise for using my word. Without me, he would have said the wrong thing. I wisely decided to keep my mouth shut. Ted never really became my friend. He tried to steal my baseball later that year and I fought him to get it back. In the movies, the fight would have caused us to respect each other and form a friendship. In reality, he waited until the next day and then smeared dog poop on my jacket. I never got any hard evidence, but I knew it was him. A kid name Jack said he had seen Ted hanging out near the jackets after recess.

I suppose it could have been Jack, trying to deflect suspicion. I later found out that Jack hated me too. I was *never* popular in that school.

The pickle jar maneuver almost succeeds. I slosh a little on my hand when I try to get the lid on. With the pickle jar back on the shelf, I get the giggles. I'm picturing the new homeowners. They will get this place at auction after I'm declared dead. They'll finish the job I started of cleaning out my uncle's possessions. Then, they'll turn their attention to the pantry.

"What a strange man," the wife will say. "Why are there rotted pickles in the graham cracker box?"

Just then, the husband will open the jar and take a whiff of what's inside.

I laugh out loud.

I stop when the tapping comes back. They're still out there, waiting for me.

(Is this how people go crazy?)

Is this how people go crazy?

I've always enjoyed time alone. Sitting solo at a restaurant never bothered me. Going to the movies by myself is a treat. I don't understand people who don't enjoy the silence of their own company. At least I never understood them until now.

The tapping has stopped again. If I shift my position against the door or even cough, I know it will come. I've revised my opinion. It's not some kind of echolocation. The tapping is meant to make me crazy so that I will run out of the pantry and into their teeth. Either that or they're trying to hypnotize me.

I can't imagine how many hours I've been in here.

The light from the truck fire has gone out. The smell of the burned truck is horrible.

For a while, I hoped that someone might see the flames from a distance and call the fire department. Then I thought that the power company might come to investigate the outage. I've given up on both of those. Out here, they rely on the residents to report things like vehicle fires and downed power lines. We're expected to be self-sufficient.

One summer, when my mom came up to spend a long weekend with us, we all went to the lake. She was horrified when Uncle Walt took off his overalls and started wading into the water.

"What happened to your leg?" she demanded.

Uncle Walt looked down. For a moment, he looked just as shocked as she was.

"Oh. I cut it."

I had seen the scar already. It was a jagged purple line on the side of his shin where the skin was puckered and the muscle bunched in funny ways when he walked. I hadn't thought anything of it. Mom seemed both disgusted and fascinated.

"Cut it? It looks like you split your whole leg in two."

"Yeah," he said with a bemused laugh. "I guess I did. It will be fine."

He waded in and swam away, closing the subject.

I didn't bring it up again until Mom had gone back south.

"Did you really split your leg open?"

He nodded. "Yup."

"Who fixed it up for you?"

He glanced down, like the answer might come from his flesh.

"Nobody. I just pushed everything back into place and wrapped it up. The body knows what to do if you let it. If I had seen a doctor, they probably would have cut it off."

"But what happened?"

"Fell off the ladder," he said.

Uncle Walt was always comfortable on a ladder. After his knee started to give him trouble, he was almost too comfortable up there. On the top rung, he would shake and rattle the ladder to a new position instead of climbing down to move it over a few inches.

"My foot got hung up in the rungs when I tumbled and I split my calf."

That was enough information for me. At the time, I figured that he had been too embarrassed to seek help. Whenever I hid an injury, that was always why. I never wanted to admit that I had done something stupid and needed help. But later, as I thought about Uncle Walt at his funeral, I realized that he *enjoyed* asking for help and he was never shy about admitting his own mistakes. There had to have been another reason why he had wrapped his leg himself and not told Mom about the injury. I wondered if maybe the whole thing had been a lie. There was no way to find out now.

People who live out in the country are expected to be self-sufficient. Some people take that idea way too far.

There's a box of cereal up on the shelf across from me. My leg is asleep. I stretch it out and poke around with my toe until the box topples and lands in my lap. I suppose I would make a pretty good blind person. I'm adjusting fairly easily to a world without light.

When I pop the cardboard top and find the plastic liner, I know what's going to happen when I tear it open.

"You want some of this?" I ask.

The tapping responds immediately. It's coming from both doors now—the kitchen and shed. I shake my head and sigh in the darkness before shoving dry cereal in my mouth.

"Needs milk," I say.

The tapping speeds up.

They're nothing if not consistent.

I'm startled when tapping comes through the wall to my left. They can't tap on the wall at my feet—on the other side of that is the old chimney.

"I believe you have me surrounded," I say.

(I must have fallen asleep mid-chew.)

I must have fallen asleep mid-chew.

There is cereal stuck to my lip. I wipe off my face with the back of my hand and jump when a shape passes in front of my face.

I freeze.

Wiggling my fingers, I see that the shape is my own hand.

I look down and see the dawn light leaking from under the kitchen door.

"Hello?" I whisper.

I clear my throat and wish that I had something to drink. Even the pickle juice would taste good right now.

I cough and try again.

"Hello? Are you there?"

I bang and twist against the stepladder so I can press my face to the floor and look under the crack. I see nothing but unbroken light reflecting off the floor. There are no shadows moving around. My heart thuds in my chest as I contemplate doing the unthinkable—I'm going to open the door.

"Hold on," I whisper. "Just hold on."

It looks really bright out there. My eyes have been in the dark so long that it might still, technically, be before dawn. There's no harm in waiting another minute or two to be sure.

I start counting, moving my lips so I can throw some Mississippis between the numbers to keep them spaced out. When I get to a hundred, I look again.

It seems brighter.

My heart starts thudding again.

"It's breakfast time," I say, raising my voice. "Who wants cereal?"

There's nothing—no tapping and nothing moving around in

the light.

Another idea occurs to me before I move the ladder out of the way. I dig in the bag and pull out a big handful of round cereal. Weighing them in my hand first, I chuck them at the gap under the door, sending them out into the kitchen. They're my little ambassadors, checking to see if the natives are friendly out there.

"Want any more?" I ask.

Silence.

"Want to count them?"

I throw another handful.

When I'm certain that no unnaturally-long fingers are going to pick up the pieces of cereal, I allow myself to move the ladder. Before I even think about moving the broom, I gather myself and climb to my feet. I stretch my legs and wiggle my toes inside my shoes. Every muscle has to be ready for what might be waiting.

This is it.

I pop the broom free and grip it like a weapon. My shoulder pulses with a deep ache when I squeeze.

I open the door and pull it towards me slowly, letting my eyes adjust to the morning light.

Everything is perfectly still.

I take a step—unearthing myself from my coffin.

It seems too quiet.

I take another step and glance down. There are a few big chunks of glass on the floor—blasted in with the explosion, but the small shards have all been cleaned up. The side door is ajar. I can't remember if I left it open when I fled.

I pull it open and regard the dooryard.

Uncle Walt's truck is a blackened husk. The power and utility lines look like charred serpents. I step out, free myself from the house, and run. I'm in the middle of the road before I stop.

I turn back and regard everything from this distance. I try to see it all with fresh eyes.

It looks like someone drunkenly crashed the truck into the

telephone pole, it fell, and the truck caught on fire. That's what I would guess.

My notebook is still there, beyond the truck. The body is gone. The one that cut my gas line and burned up in the explosion has been taken away or turned to dust. Without any evidence, one guess is as good as the other.

It's starting to occur to me that I need to form a plan. In the best-case scenario, I can walk up to Mr. Engel's and use his phone. The house is probably locked up now, but I'll get in. I think Amber will understand. I don't have any identification and my cellphone is lost somewhere in the grass on the other side of the barn. All that is secondary.

I take a step backwards. I've taken the first step towards Mr. Engel's house.

If I can get out of here in one piece and get back to sanity, it's a win.

Is it though?

Does getting out of here in one piece put a tick in the W column?

What happens after that?

I'll need my driver's license, birth certificate, or passport at some point. All those things are in Uncle Walt's house. What am I going to do, ask the police to go inside with me? That will require a story of some sort. I'll have to say that someone tried to break in and then what? Do I say that I crashed the truck? They're going to suspect that I was drinking. Do I care?

But, seriously, what's next after that?

Am I going to try to sell the house as it stands now?

What happens when the realtor tries to show the house and the prospective buyers ask to see the cellar? What are they going to find down there?

Light

(I start with the notebook.)

I start with the notebook.

I add the following:

"Listen—you can call me crazy if you want to, but I was attacked. I crashed the truck, but _they_ cut the fuel line. They were the same ones from Mr. Engel's cellar. I'm well aware of how this sounds, but I believe they were _vampires_. Call them what you like, but I believe they were parasitic predators, trying to feed from my blood. If that's not a vampire, I don't know what is. I spent all night locked in the pantry while they tapped on the doors. Now, I'm going to _take my house back_."

My hand is cramped from squeezing the pencil. The hasty text is barely legible.

I toss the notebook in the driveway and approach the house.

This is my uncle's house, regardless of what currently infests it. One could argue that they might have fled in the night to find a better place to roost, but I _know_ they're here. I can sense it.

I know something else, too—I know they can die.

Standing back, I reach forward and shove the key into

David's door. It goes easily this time and I turn the handle. I push it open with the broom. The hinges creak. Light spills into the hall and I lean forward to look right, left, and up. Next stop is the sliding door. With that open, the shed has a decent amount of light. I head for the woodshop and glance around under the dusty counters before I get to work.

I use a handsaw and chisel to sharpen both the end of the broom stick and a shovel handle that Uncle Walt was saving.

When Mom would make cookies, she would hand me two, saying, "One for each hand."

I'm holding two sharpened stakes.

"One for each hand," I whisper to myself.

My should feels limber and strong even when I squeeze the broom handle hard.

I feel ready.

As I move through the shed, I close doors behind me. I cross the floor of the barn fast and unlock the big doors to throw them open. Light rolls into the lower floor of the barn.

If feels like something is missing as the dust swirls in the shafts of morning light.

All the stalls are empty. Uncle Walt lost or gave away all of his animals before he became too frail to care for them. I would like to see it filled again—a winter refuge for cows, sheep, goats, and horses. The barn was a perfect tiny ecosystem.

I work my way from one stall to the next, checking every corner. I inspect the milk room, standing back as I lift the lid of the old cooler in there. I look under the stairs, making sure no hands will shoot out and trip me up before I climb, and then I peer around the lofts.

When I'm satisfied that the barn is empty, I turn back for the house.

Searching the barn and shed were a formality, really. I didn't expect to find anything there. I needed a warmup.

I'm back at the pantry door. The last thing I want to do is step through that space again. It doesn't feel so bad when I open the door from the shed. The space is infused with kitchen light now. The endless black expanse of it has been returned to reality.

I step through.

There's enough light in the kitchen now that I can see tiny glints from the floor. When they cleaned up the glass, they missed the slivers. Flies are already buzzing near the fridge and I smell something sweet over there. It's no surprise. Uncle Walt's refrigerator isn't as old as Mr. Engel's, and it doesn't have a hard latch on the door. Without power for a night, the food in there is probably already spoiling.

I use my stakes to flip open the biggest of the cabinets and even some of the smaller ones.

The kitchen is clear.

I mean, aside from the cellar door, it's clear. I'm saving that for last.

Before I leave, I turn back and have second thoughts. It's not enough to keep it closed, but I slide the table over from its normal spot over so I can push it against the cellar door. A strong hand could shove it aside, but I'll hear the noise if they do.

I grab a flashlight from the hall closet and tape it to the broom handle. I can point the light and jab with the same hand if I need to. The rest of the first floor doesn't take much time. There aren't that many hiding places aside from two closets and under the table in the dining room. I pull the tablecloth like a magician and get ready to jab. There's nothing there.

The only evidence I see of them consists of smeared fingerprints on the windows. Leaning close, I try to make out swirls and circles in the oil. Their prints don't look like ours at all. It almost looks like the marks were made by scales. That revelation sends a shudder through me. I'm not a big fan of snakes.

Uncle Walt always used to say, "They can't hear you screaming at them like that, and if they can, they don't understand you."

It didn't stop me from yelling every time I lifted a bucket

and found a coiled snake underneath.

"There are no venomous snakes up here," my uncle would always say. It didn't matter. I wasn't reacting out of a fear of envenomation. The fear was fundamental. It still is. I don't even like watching snakes on TV. The way they move is unnatural.

I'm standing here at the bottom of the stairs, lost in memory, because I'm afraid of what I might find on the second floor. The bedrooms upstairs are supposed to be safe. If I find something up there, I'll never be able to fall asleep in this home again.

I tap my sharpened stake on a stair tread and take a step.

          (I swear I heard something.)

I swear I heard something.

The room next to the bathroom is the one that Uncle Walt always used to call "Grandma's room." When Mom would come to visit, he would say, "You can take your mother's things up to Grandma's room, of course."

That would cause Mom to make a face and backhand Uncle Walt while he feigned injury.

Uncle Walt was thirteen months younger than Mom.

My uncle would hold up a bulb before he changed it, and say something to her like, "When you were my age, did they have these fancy lightbulbs?"

Mom always gave him the same dry laugh. In every way, Mom seemed much younger than Uncle Walt, but the comments about her age always offended her.

I can see under the bed in Grandma's room from the stairs. That's one hiding spot I can check off the list.

I start with the bathroom, sweeping aside the shower curtain and jabbing into the empty space. I look behind the door and declare the room clear. In Grandma's room, I look in the wardrobe and see the clothes that I've managed to forget about.

Mom always left clothes up here for her visits so she wouldn't have to travel with a big suitcase. Back at home, she went through clothes pretty fast. Using Goodwill like her extended closet, she cycled outfits for the season and her changing moods. Up here, she wore a pretty consistent uniform.

"What does it matter?" she would say. "There's nobody up here worth looking good for."

"Not at your age," Uncle Walt would say.

That would earn him another hit.

Grandma's room doesn't have a closet. It's quickly finished.

I move on to Uncle Walt's room.

His room is still filled with mysteries. With my broom handle, I lift the skirt on his bed and peer underneath. This seems like a horrible invasion of his privacy, even though I only find dust bunnies under there. I haven't even started to empty out this room. I've been leaving it for last.

Uncle Walt never hesitated to answer any direct question, but he still seemed like a very private man.

On one visit—I must have been in my early twenties—we were sitting at the kitchen table when I finally got up enough nerve to ask, "How come you never had a girlfriend... or a boyfriend?"

He smiled and laughed.

"I did. Once. It ended poorly and I decided that, for me, the risk wasn't worth the reward."

"What risk? Getting your heart broken if it doesn't work out?"

He shook his head. "No. Not that. Infection."

I misunderstood at first. I thought he was talking about literal infection, like something sexually transmitted. He must have grasped that his statement could have been misconstrued because he immediately clarified.

"Heartbreak is finite for most people. It's like a cracked rib. The pain is terrible, but you don't even have to put a cast on it. It wouldn't do any good. After a while, the pain subsides and you're good as new. For me, a heartbreak is a compound fracture. My internals pierce through the skin and let all kinds of pathogens in. Last time, I realized that the next break would likely kill me."

He had weaponized his own metaphor and used it to put a cap on his own joy.

I told him as much.

Uncle Walt agreed with me. That was the frustrating part with him sometimes. You could point out his hypocrisy and he would listen thoughtfully. Then, instead of changing his behavior, he would simply agree and keep on doing whatever he was doing.

I pull open one of his closet doors and look at the hanging clothes for a moment before I push them aside with my stake and probe the corners with the flashlight beam. These clothes still hold his shape. The hanging overalls bulge out in the middle and I can see the mouth of the pocket where his hooked thumb stretched the seam.

I check the other closet. This one holds a dresser with tall drawers. I shine the flashlight on either side to make sure that nothing is hiding in the gaps.

My room is next.

The sheets and thin bedspread are swirled and tossed.

Uncle Walt always insisted that I make the bed each morning.

"It makes a world of difference in how you greet the day," he said. "Night is for wild dreams and disorder. Put everything in its place when you wake up and you'll have a different outlook on life. Try it and see."

I had and I did. Ever since, I had made my bed each morning. The action is robotic, and it gives me a chance to prepare myself for what I'm going to do that day. It's strange to see my bed in such disorder. I can't blame this on anyone but myself. I left the bed in a hurry when they knocked on the door.

I check under the bed, in the closet, and behind the door.

This room is clear too, but I know I heard something when I climbed the stairs.

That leaves only one possibility.

I stand under the trapdoor that leads up to the attic. I've been up there a few times. When Uncle Walt installed cable TV, he ran it up to the attic next to the old chimney and then had me fish it down through the wall. It's all blown-in insulation up there. It makes my skin itch just thinking about it.

Those scaly vampires probably don't mind the insulation, but I don't know how they deal with the heat up there. As I remember, it's stuffy and hot as hell. If they're up there, Mr. Engel must have been wrong about them hating the heat.

With a couple of failed attempts, I use the tip of one of my spears to hook the ring and I pull down the trapdoor. The springs groan out a warning and then it clangs into place. A thick chunk of pink insulation comes down with the stairs. I nudge it to the side and it falls silently to the floor. I circle underneath warily, pointing the beam up into the darkness above. For a moment, I think I catch a glimpse of glowing eyes. It's just the flashlight reflecting off of something metal though. I reach up and unfold the stairs.

Going up there is a terrible idea.

They could easily surprise me from behind as I ascend above the level of the attic floor. They might even hide in the loose insulation and snatch me from below.

Aside from the cellar, this is the last place to check.

I hold my breath and climb.


```
(With every step, I feel the temperature

            increase.)
```


With every step, I feel the temperature increase.

Dust swirls in the beam of my light.

I'm looking at the underside of rafters that were hoisted into place more than a hundred and fifty years before I was born. I have no way to guess the age of what I'm hunting. In books and movies, vampires survive to an incredible age. I'm not sure why that's the case. You never hear about werewolves living eternally. How come only vampires have learned to cheat death?

When my head breaches the level of the attic, I spin and aim my light at the corners where the rafters meet the walls. My quick inspection reveals nothing, but I know that there are plenty of hidden nooks up there. I spent more than my fair share of time running cables. Uncle Walt dressed me up like a mummy before he sent me up. I had to wear long sleeves, gloves, a breathing mask, and goggles before I climbed.

Today, I have jeans and a t-shirt.

I can still see the depression in the insulation from the last time I stepped across these beams. There's nothing to walk on but the spines of the beams that are buried in the insulation. Uncle Walt trusted me not to slip and put my foot down through the ceiling. He warned me a lot, and then he trusted me.

I put a cautious foot down and feel around until I'm sure that it's planted firmly on a beam. These beams were cut up on the hill from old-growth fir trees according to Uncle Walt. It bends under my weight. That didn't happen twenty years ago.

I hear a creak and whip around to see the source. It's just the wood complaining about my presence. With another careful step, I can nearly see around the corner into the space behind the chimney. Before Uncle Walt put on the metal roof, he busted the top off of the unused chimney. Now it ends here in the attic. This ancient ruin is evidence of the house's original heart.

I'm holding my breath as I lean to get a look.

There's nothing there.

In the daylight, with no real evidence of them, it's easy to dismiss that I ever saw them. I'm not going to make that mistake. They were here. My uncle's truck is burned up and I spent the night in the pantry. I'm not going to forget what I saw.

I start working my way back to the other side. From the outside of the house, the roof looks pretty consistent. Up here, I can see evidence of the alterations that the house has gone through. The original building ended just ahead of me.

Grandma's room and the upstairs bath were a part of an addition. I point my flashlight through a hole the size of an old window and look into the slightly newer section.

The cable is draped through the hole, right where I ran it. This is where I lost my balance and nearly fell through the ceiling when I was a kid.

I have to set down one of my stakes to step through.

My shoelace catches on a nail or something, and it almost happens. I teeter for a moment and then get a hand on a rafter to steady myself.

I'm breathing hard—taking the attic dust deep into my lungs.

There's only one more spot to check.

My eyes are locked on a place where the roof seems to absorb the light coming from my flashlight. My foot is trying to find the next beam.

Uncle Walt said that a fire in the bathroom nearly burned the place down in the forties. The only evidence of that blaze is up here, in the attic. Surrounding the iron pipe, the beams and rafters are all charred. More wood was added to stabilize the structure.

I don't see anything.

I angle my beam slightly, just to make sure.

As I turn away, something shifts there, where the wood is blackened.

All I see are the charred beams and planks.

When the eye opens, and I see the blue glow, I understand. It's camouflaged.

My terror is immediately put on hold as I contemplate the eye.

It's wrong to think of it as a glow. The eye doesn't emit light, really. It's a portal into another realm, where darkness doesn't exit. Clear blue sky and happiness are the only things that exist in that place beyond the eye. If I only allow it, I will slip into that world and every care and concern will melt away.

I want nothing more than that, and it's mine for the taking.

All I have to do is accept the eye and peace will be mine forever.

My foot slips and my weight comes down on the strapping that the ceiling below is attached to. It cracks and gives, but I don't fall through.

At the sound, the eye turns from me and I'm lost.

My perfect world was a lie.

For one second, everything is clear and I thrust with my stake. I don't aim for the chest, trying to pierce the heart. I don't even know if it has a heart. All I know is the eye. I can't risk being captured by that eye again so that's what I aim for.

It doesn't even try to move.

I did a poor job of sharpening the end of the broomstick. It doesn't matter. The pointed wood easily slides into the eye and the illusion pops with a gush of fluid. The thing screams and thrashes, but it's pinned into place at the end of the broomstick.

As it twists in agony, the camouflage illusion disappears.

I see the other eye, or what's left of it. The lid is crusted down with thick slime. It must have suffered some past injury that took half of its potency. I'm lucky for that. One stake is enough to dispatch it.

The wriggling stops but the fluid doesn't stop pulsing out from around my stake.

The thing is withering. It appears like it's made entirely of liquid and it's all leaking out around the hole I made with the stake. I don't understand the physics of it—how something solid can turn itself inside out and melt like that.

The ceiling cracks under my foot again and I snap back to reality.

I push up and away, retracting back through the passage back to the main part of the attic. I'm coughing the dust out of my lungs as I stumble back down the stairs.

I'm no longer sure that my inspection of the house was thorough. I'm not longer sure of anything.

(I find the second one.)

I find the second one.

It's in the space behind the dresser in Uncle Walt's closet.

I can't even imagine how it fit back there.

When I came down from the attic, I didn't even have a real plan. I started poking my stakes into every dark corner, regardless of whether or not I saw anything. Back in Uncle Walt's room, I lifted one of my stakes to a high angle and shoved it back behind the dresser in the closet. It met resistance and I heard something shifting around back there. I tossed the drawers onto my uncle's bed and pulled out the dresser enough so I can get access.

Without looking, I take the sharpened shovel handle in both hands and start driving it down into the darkness back there.

With the first few stabs, it tries to slip and dodge. I must have hit something vital because it stops moving. I keep driving the stake down anyway and the solid flesh gives way and I hear the stake sloshing into something squishy.

I'm not as dumb as I look. I don't peer over the edge of the dresser just yet. Instead, I find a new angle and pump the stake again until I find another pocket of resistance. Something screams this time and I stab at it blindly until my arms ache and there's clearly nothing left of it.

When I pull the dresser out, I see a pool of gore.

It's evaporating into thick smoke that hugs the floor.

I back up fast so I don't inhale any.

It takes several careful minutes before I'm willing to claim that Uncle Walt's room is clear. I go back to Grandma's room and then the bathroom. They're clear as well.

Back in my room, I already have a sense of where to look.

The way the end tables bracket the bed, they create a shadow that's right underneath where I lay my head. I kneel next to the bed like I'm getting ready to pray.

With my good arm, I bang the end of the stake into the shadows.

This one is crafty. It's moving around, trying to avoid the stake. I press my face agains the side of the mattress and maneuver the broomstick so I can reach the far corner. When I feel something with the end of the stake, I commit even more to the reach.

That's when it almost gets me.

Talons grab my wrist and pull. I can feel the claws dig into my skin and I shriek. This was so stupid. I know how much they hate the light. Why didn't I just dismantle the bed? I could have pulled off the mattress and thrown it into the hall. I could have carried the end tables away and given it no place to hide.

It tugs with incredible strength and I feel my elbow pop and the bones in my wrist grind together.

My other hand fumbles and finally closes around the broomstick. When I shove that into the darkness, I finally hit the thing. It screams and the grip on my wrist weakens. I jump on the opportunity, stabbing both stakes into the space under the bed while I prop myself up by pressing my forehead against the bed's wooden frame.

One of the stakes meets the resistance of soft tissue and I use that to pin it in place while I jab with the other. The screams finally stop and I can help myself. I lower my head to see the remains before they melt away. I'm hoping that it's the one with the violet eyes. That's what got me into this.

The fading eyes are green.

I pierce them with the stakes and watch the face turn to goo before it dissolves.

When I was up on the roof of the barn, being chased across the shingles, I thought that they almost had a human shape. Sure, they moved in a strange way, but they still had arms, legs, a torso, and a head. I'm beginning to think that was more camouflage.

Their real shape can only be seen in that moment between

death and melting. They're more of a serpent or reptile than anything else.

When it has melted away and I push back up to my knees, I take a good look at the wrist. The claws punctured into my skin. I can only imagine what kind of infections they might carry. I drop both stakes and rush for the bathroom.

Uncle Walt kept a big bottle of alcohol in the cabinet. I spin off the cap and pour the contents over my wounds. The sting is white hot pain, rocketing up my arm. My flesh bubbles and foams and then the alcohol runs clear.

I don't know if that did anything or not.

I press a hand towel against my wrist until the burning stops and I look at the oozing blood. In the movies, a person bitten by a vampire is doomed to become one themselves. They never talk about puncture wounds from the claws. I guess that means that there's no danger.

"Ha," I say.

(The next one is roosting.)

The next one is roosting.

I find it in the top of the coat closet off the living room. Beyond the shoe boxes on the shelf, there's a dark place up there and it has found a way to cling to the ceiling. Maybe they have some kind of sticky feet, like a salamander or something. I don't see anything. When I poke my stick, I feel it up there. I squeeze my eyes shut—there's no way to tell where its hypnotic eyes might be—and I stab upwards. The beam of the flashlight smears red against my eyelids whenever I pull back.

It drops from the assault and I stumble backwards over a stack of books.

There's a patch of sunlight reflected off the glass door of the china cabinet. It drops into that light and shrieks. When I hear that sound, I immediately remember the smell of the burning truck. Those two senses are linked in my memory.

I thrust a stake at the green eyes when they turn on me. This one has a scarred, stretched-out neck. One eye pops and I get the other one as the thing writhes in agony. I'm not sure if it's the light or the stabbing that kills it, but it is an evaporating puddle of disgusting slime before long.

How many is that?

I've exterminated four, I believe. I wish I knew how many I was hunting. The one thing I know for sure is that I haven't yet seen the one with violet eyes. Unless the color of the eyes changes. I suppose I can't rule that out.

This is purely instinctual, but hear me out—I've come to think of the one with violet eyes as female. What if they're like a hive of bees and she is the queen? The ones that I've been dispatching might be the drones or something.

That would be too easy.

My compulsion is to look for definitive solutions to things.

I'm constructing a narrative where I can wipe out all of the vampires just by killing the one with the violet eyes. I'm trying to establish her as the boss or mother.

I shake my head, banishing the thought. Even if I find the one with the violet eyes, I can't assume that I'm safe. That would be foolish.

I stand in the kitchen, waving at flies. They must be coming in through the broken windows. I'm staring at the cellar door. There are no windows down there. The only light will be what I bring with me. Based on what nearly happened under my bed, this is a recipe for disaster.

I can't use this cellar door the stairs beyond it.

There is one another option. Before I head outside, I move the table aside so I can make an escape up the cellar stairs if I have to.

It's already getting hot outside and the sun is still low in the sky.

I don't even bother trying to lift the handle of the bulkhead doors. I locked them from the inside. Hopefully, the hasp on the door isn't very strong. Uncle Walt has a long steel bar that he used to use to lift the corner of the garden tractor when it was time for an oil change. I shove that under the corner of the door and lift.

Pain flares through my shoulder and I remember Uncle Walt.

One time we were trying to lift one of the barn doors a few inches so we could put a new roller on the top. I couldn't lift it with the bar. He pointed and said, "Use your assets."

When he positioned a block of wood under the bar as a fulcrum, I thought that the asset he was referring to was my brain. It wasn't. He meant for me to stand on the bar—using my weight to lift instead of my muscles.

I roll a big rock into place near the bulkhead and position the bar. When I step onto the long end, the door lifts and the hasp pops free.

The hinges screech and I remember the smell of burning truck. A shaft of light cuts into the dark cellar and shows me a small patch of the gravel floor.

I have another idea.

When I come back out, I have three mirrors from the house. They reflect the sun back into my face as I descend. When I get to the bottom, I arrange the mirrors in the sunlight so they can reflect into the corners of the cellar.

The cellar used to have windows built into the foundation of the house. The panes were so thin and brittle that Uncle Walt decided to do away with them. He ended up just boarding up the holes. With apologies to his craftsmanship, I swing the blunt end of his steel bar at the nearest window hole and break through the planks. With a few good hits, more sunlight is streaming into cellar. I do the other window on that side. It's not worth doing the ones on the other side of the house—the sun won't hit those until this afternoon.

I pick up my two stakes and glance at the flashlight to make sure it's still on and working.

This is it.

It occurs to me that I don't have to go through with this.

I got one last night when the truck exploded and I mushed up four of them in the house. Maybe that's fair? Mr. Engel and one truck for five of them? Of course, I would still be stuck with not having a place to stay and selling my uncle's place without finishing the job of cleaning it.

All the pros and cons still exist, but the question remains: have I satisfied my need for revenge?

I look down at my wrist where the punctures have pretty much closed. It's not a terrible injury. I don't need retribution for it or anything. But it irks me that these things exist at all. That alone is enough reason for me to try to finish this job. People are not supposed to be prey. This is not only about defending my uncle's property. This is about eradicating a threat to our primacy as a species.

I stand tall with this thought and I start down through the bulkhead doors.

Shadows

(This is the hardest thing I've ever done.)

This is the hardest thing I've ever done.

I've buried my mom, my wife, our baby, and my uncle. I've endured a lot of grief. That trauma was thrust upon me. I didn't have to walk down the stairs into that pain with open eyes, like I'm doing now.

Sunlight cuts through the cellar in places. By bashing out the boarded up windows and placing the mirrors, I've created a few shafts of light. I'm not sure it was the best idea. The bright light makes the shadows even deeper. Every dark spot seems to crawl with shifting shapes. I'm almost certain it's just an artifact of the contrast.

Almost certain.

In comparison to the sunlight, my flashlight beam is barely visible.

I start at the nearest corner and begin working my way around the cellar, poking my stakes into the shadows.

I find one almost immediately.

With my first stab, the eyes open and clawed fingers reach towards me. They halt when they get to the shaft of sunlight. With all the dazzling light around, the eyes fail to entrance me. I can study the orange irises. They're like two flames. Their gaze tries to entrance me closer, so I'll be out of the light. I'm finding it easy to keep my wits and resist. There's a chance that I'm just growing accustomed to the hypnosis now. This one has deep scars on its wrist, like it tried to reach through a broken window.

I smile and send my two stakes at the eyes.

It doesn't even blink before they make contact. Right until the end, it was trying to catch me with its hypnotic gaze.

When it screams out its final sounds, I hear shifting around me. There are more down here. Maybe a lot more.

I find another under the oil tank. Its green eyes narrow as it regards me. Once the eyes are open, it's a lot easier to see the whole body. The camouflage illusion fades and I can see the way that it's clinging to the bottom of the oil tank. I wonder if it doesn't have the energy to camouflage and hypnotize at the same time. Maybe it doesn't feel the need to do both.

A third attempts to creep up while I'm watching the one under the oil tank turn to slime.

My feet are in shadow and it almost wraps its talons around my ankle.

It freezes when I turn. It's like we were playing a game of Red Light, Green Light and I spun just in time to stall its progress. The yellow eyes flicker with hate until I stab them. Is it hate though? I don't want to attribute emotions to these things. As far as I know, they're just clever animals.

That's three down here, four from the house, and one burned up with the truck. Eight total, so far, and I haven't seen the one with violet eyes. It occurs to me that I didn't see the eyes of the one that burned up in the dooryard. Could that be the one I'm looking for?

I'm trying to remember—what were the color of the eyes that I saw in the shed when I went in through David's door?

The question vexes me while I continue to search.

I'm almost convinced that I'm done when I find two more in the far corner. These two weren't trying to attack, like the yellow-eyed devil. They both have orange eyes. While I'm jabbing one with the stake, the other creeps forward.

The wide eyes almost look like they have spiral galaxies trapped in their pulsing light. I wish I had my phone. It would be fascinating to take a picture of those eyes and really study them. Could they be wormholes that lead to another solar system? Is it an illusion, or are they actually as deep as they look?

Someone else will have to answer that question.

I'm content with driving my spear into the eye.

It flinches back from the flashlight, hissing when the beam strikes its skin. Colors flash through the scales. I impale it with my stake.

The total stands at ten.

I want to take a break.

I have to keep going though. If I lose my nerve now, I might not find it again.

I go back to the start. None of this means anything if I'm not thorough.

Standing in the middle of the mirrors, I close my eyes. With one of the stakes, I reach up and tap on a beam, trying to replicate the rhythm that they make with their claws.

My eyes fly open when I hear something. I see exactly where the sound came from.

It makes perfect sense.

The thing is over near the stairs. I should have guessed. They're smart enough to know that it was likely I was going to come down that way, so they hid a sentinel near the stairs to grab me when I came down. While I'm trying to puzzle out exactly where the head is, I notice something else.

They're well camouflaged to match their surroundings, but they can't bend light. When my flashlight beam lands directly on it, I don't really see anything. Held at a steep angle, the shadows give it away. I sense a strange parallax when the light hits it at an angle.

I probe it with a stake until I see the eyes and then I stab it.

Blue—the eyes were blue.

That makes eleven. The cellar is clear.

Now that they're all gone, I can feel the difference. The dread I felt has evaporated along with the slime. I stand for a full minute, looking at the way the sunlight swirls through the dust. It's beautiful. Sunlight is the best disinfectant, right?

The cellar looks almost too clean.

"Spiders," I whisper.

That's the problem—where are the spiders?

Sometimes, I can be pretty dense. I run for the stairs.

(I search my senses.)

I search my senses.

There's no feeling of dread in here. I'm standing in the barn, looking up at the loft because of the revelation I had in the cellar. The vampires must eat spiders. I didn't see any spiders in Mr. Engel's basement, and I didn't see any in my cellar. These are places that definitely should have spiders. Maine is famous for giant, fat-bodied spiders. At least in my family it always was. Mom would complain about them all the time and Uncle Walt would always defend them.

"They don't do any harm and they eat tons of mosquitoes," he would always say.

The barn, in particular, was home to some giant arachnids. I never liked them much, but I left them alone in deference to my uncle.

But now I can't see a single web. My flashlight doesn't reveal any at all.

I also can't find any evidence of the vampires though. There's no sense of dread and my light isn't doing any of the parallax shifting that I discovered. The siding of the barn is so inconsistent that the place is full of random shafts of sunlight now. Once the sun came up fully over the horizon, it riddled the barn with ambient light.

I make a thorough search of the first floor and then climb to the loft.

Granted, I can't reach the highest peaks. I set up the flashlight to point to various spots and then I move away from that light source so I can see everything from different angles. There's just no way. Even with their camouflage, I would see them if they were here.

At one point, they had to be here. That's the only way to explain the lack of spiders. Maybe they roosted up here for a bit during the night. Some of them waited here while the others tried to tap me out of the pantry. After that, the bulk of them must have moved to the cellar where there was less light.

I don't know—it's a theory.

I comb through the barn several times, trying to find them. It's like looking for my keys when I'm late for an appointment. I know exactly what they should look like, but there's no trace of them. I have to force myself to slow down and really *see* the barn.

I'm sweaty and dusty by the time I'm sitting on the stairs and I admit defeat.

"Maybe that's all of them," I say.

It doesn't feel true. I had this weird sense of dread when I was close to one in the house. It's like that skin-crawling feel when someone is staring at the back of my head. I'm not getting that feeling out in the barn, but I still can't help but think that I'm missing something.

The flashlight beam is still strong. Uncle Walt replaced the bulbs in all his flashlights a few years ago. The new bulbs emit a really harsh light compared to the old ones, but they last forever now.

Sweeping the light around aimlessly, I catch one corner of a spiderweb above me. The spider is gone and the web won't be rebuilt. That's a shame. I bet the whole barn will be swarming with flies before long. I can only hope that the spiders return quickly.

"Flies," I whisper.

I stand up slowly.

"Why are there so many flies in the kitchen?" I ask.

All the spiders are gone, sure, but why did I see flies in the kitchen but nowhere else? I'm walking pretty fast towards the shed. I force myself to slow down and take my time. I can't assume anything. My gut doesn't give me any warnings, but it would be stupid to trust that alone.

Holding the flashlight away from myself at an angle, I check the shadowy corners of the shed hall as I move towards the kitchen.

I step through he pantry fast—that place still feels like a prison cell to me. I don't want to be incarcerated again.

For a moment, I don't see a single fly. I'm about to admit that maybe I was wrong, but then my skin starts to crawl. Something is here.

That's whey I spot the flies. They're still there, over by the refrigerator. I sidestep a wide arc around the appliance. The flies are concentrated by the back of it. I shine my light.

The first thing I see is the corner of one of the metal racks from the interior of the fridge. Stuffed between the rack and refrigerator body is a pack of hamburger buns.

I creep forward and see a plastic bottle of ketchup and then the husk of an ear of corn.

There wasn't much food in there. I have been eating mostly from the pantry. I'm guessing that everything that I had in the refrigerator is now stuffed behind it.

The flies buzz in an angry cloud when I reach my stake forward and poke at the hamburger buns.

Something shifts inside the fridge.

(The door won't open.)

The door won't open.

I try to wedge my stake into the rubber seal between the refrigerator door and the frame, but I can't get it to budge. When

I bang my stake against the fridge in frustration, I hear the thing inside. It shifts and the scales rub against each other making a dry, papery sound. When I hear that sound, my wrist throbs. It looks like the claw wound is weeping again.

I put one of the stakes down and slink forward until my trembling hand grabs the towel that's tied to the refrigerator's handle. The whole time, all I can picture is the door sliding open and long boney fingers slipping out to snare me.

I get a grip on the towel and back away.

With my first tug, the refrigerator actually rocks forward a little.

The second time, I really jerk it.

The towel starts to rip and then the door pops open.

For a second, I don't see a single thing inside there. Someone has emptied the refrigerator and left it bare. Maybe it was just the vacuum that made it so difficult to open.

I know better than that. I circle at a distance until I can pick up the broomstick with the flashlight taped to it and get a good angle.

That's when I see her. She's up near the top corner, clinging to the plastic. When you really get a good look at them, they're pretty small. She's the size of a small alligator, I would guess. Her eyes make her look human. They're such an amazing violet color.

I think I read that in ancient Europe, only royalty could wear purple. If that color was anything like this, I understand. The color of her eyes suggests infinite wealth and prosperity. It conveys a feel of deep satisfaction. Even with the sunlight dazzling through the broken windows, her eyes are bright.

Her eyes invite me to come inside the refrigerator. It will be our safe place as soon as I crawl inside and shut the door. Who needs light and oxygen? I'll have complete happiness in there. Why would I possibly want anything else?

I take a step forward.

With my next step, I drop the stake that I fashioned out of the shovel handle.

I'm still holding the broomstick with the flashlight taped to it, but I let the light droop. I don't need it anymore. There's plenty of light coming from her perfect violet eyes.

The eyes seem to grow even larger with my next step.

It's like they're swallowing my whole field of vision, and that's a wonderful thing.

Violet is the overwhelming color, but the eyes are actually made up of a billion points of light, like tiny stars in swirling galaxies. There's an entire reality inside those eyes and it's a perfect existence. Some people believe in reincarnation. If they could see her eyes, those people would understand that coming back to this life would be torture. The only afterlife I want is to be encompassed in that beauty.

Her mouth opens and I see the dripping fangs. It doesn't matter. Those teeth are waiting to bite me and I really couldn't care less. She's welcome to this mortal flesh as long as that payment grants me entrance to the universe inside her violet eyes.

Light can't last forever. Darkness always wins.

I don't know where that thought came from, but it conjures an image for me. The invading image is Kimberly. It's not the last memory I have of Kimberly with agony stretching her face. I had a handful of ice chips melting between my fingers as I watched them prep her for surgery. Whenever I think of her name, that's what I always picture, but that's not the image that comes to me now.

Instead, what I see is Kimberly on the day that she told me she was pregnant. I was in a terrible mood that day, and she held up the stick that she had peed on—the pregnancy test with its blue plus sign. She said, "Your darkness can't last forever. Light always wins."

Somewhere along the way, I reversed her words.

My version is clearly more true.

I take another step. I'm going to join that violet paradise in the refrigerator. That universe fills my eyes and banishes the memory of Kimberly that I had conjured.

A brilliant light glares from my right and I'm blinded by it. I stagger to the side, but I'm still assaulted by the beam. It's a reflection in the glass that's stacked on the windowsill. The blast from the truck broke the window, the vampire's OCD forced it to collect the glass, and now it has reflected the sun into my eyes and broken the violet spell that entranced me.

I blink at the sunlight and glance back at the refrigerator.

For a fraction of a second, I see her for the disgusting serpent that she is. She's part snake and part lizard. Her teeth are dripping with saliva and bacteria. She's a parasite.

And then her eyes find me again.

I want nothing more than...

The sun interrupts the thought. I'm saved by that beam of light.

I raise one hand to block my view of her eyes and I raise the broomstick stake in the other. The flashlight reflects oily rainbows on her scales. She's not even trying to camouflage herself anymore. All her energy is invested in hypnotizing me with her violet eyes, but I can't see them anymore.

I aim the stake without seeing the target.

I thrust it forward.

I hear and feel the supple give of her flesh as the stake drives home.

She screeches and thrashes and I pull back and stab again.

One eye has burst. The other searches wildly for some way to escape. The refrigerator is her only refuge from the sunlight in the kitchen. She can't avoid my attack.

When I finally hit the second eye, her body convulses and begins the process of liquifying. She melts around the wooden shaft of the broomstick.

"I'm going to need a new fridge," I whisper.

The slime bubbles and evaporates. The evil mist rolls from the bottom of the refrigerator and I step back from it as it dissipates.

"Twelve."

I've removed twelve of them. I finally found the one I

thought of as the leader, and it rings true. She was the most powerful of them. The sinister feeling that pervaded the kitchen is nearly gone.

(It's nearly gone.)

It's *nearly* gone.

I have one more place to check.

The freezer door opens easily. There's no camouflage at all to the serpent that I find there, curled up with the melting ice. Of course, all I can think about is the ice chips that I was supplying to Kimberly. It was the last act of kindness I could give her, while she was giving everything to our child.

The violet-eyed monster was female. I'm sure of it now. It was female and this is the child that she died trying to protect.

When I move closer, the baby's eyes open. It's too young to try to hypnotize me. The eyes are slightly more blue than its mother's. They're still beautiful. This little one will grow up to be just as powerful as its mother, I'm sure of that.

Without another thought, I stab it.

If I had any power in the house, I'm sure the Mountain of Pure Rock would be playing a dramatic soundtrack to this murder.

Instead, all I hear is the pitiful cry of the baby as I pull back and stab again.

Hot tears fall from my eyes. My frustrated scream joins the voice of the baby as I try to puncture its wonderful eyes with my dull broomstick.

There is nothing worse than revenge. There is nothing more horrible than committing the murder of an infant while thinking of the senseless death of your own heart.

When it's done and the thing is melting into the cool water, I stagger back and fall into a chair.

Emptiness is all I feel. They're all gone—I'm sure of it now.

It's hot, the sun is continuing to rise in the sky, and I'm all alone in Uncle Walt's house. I'm all alone except for the buzzing flies.

Sun

(It's worth a shot.)

It's worth a shot.

Before I give up on this place, I circle the house and wander around in the shadow of the barn until I see it. I find my cellphone, but it's now simply a black rectangle made of glass, metal, and plastic. Somehow, the glass survived the fall when my cellphone tumbled from my hand. It doesn't turn on. Maybe it's just the battery.

I shove it in my pocket and then return inside.

I was upstairs earlier, but I forgot to pickup my wallet. It's no wonder—the mess in my bedroom reminds me of the struggle here. The pain in my wrist flares as I think about the talons that nearly dragged me into the darkness.

I had a lot of close calls last night.

I'm not going to let myself dwell on those right now.

Sorting through the mess of my bedroom, I find some clothes to change into. It would be nice to have a shower, but without power I don't have any running water. I clean up the best I can and exit the house through the kitchen.

Part of me wants to tidy up a few things first. The food behind the fridge is disgusting. The flies are still coming in through the broken windows. It would be monumentally stupid to hang around and I've done too many stupid things already.

I sit down on the porch and re-tie my shoes.

That poor truck. It was old when I was born. It served my uncle faithfully for all those years and then I blew it up in order to save my own skin. I guess it went out heroically. We could all hope to be so lucky.

I stand up, feeling unencumbered. I almost feel buoyant. The sun is too bright though. I wish my sunglasses hadn't burned up with the truck. Before I leave, I jog back inside and grab one of my uncle's baseball caps. It has his smell. He used some kind of pomade in his hair to tame his cowlick.

I'm finally ready. A voice in the back of my head says that this will be the last time I ever see this place.

"That's stupid," I say, shaking my head.

The whole point of risking my life last night was to defend this place.

Walking away, across the dooryard and beyond the burned truck, feels completely unnatural. I don't know if I can explain why. I want to turn around again, just to get one last look at the place, but I force myself to keep my eyes on the road ahead. Once I'm over the hill and my uncle's place is out of sight, I wish I had.

(This is the house that started it all.)

This is the house that started it all.

Walking to Mr. Engel's, I've had some time to meditate on what I might find. First, I have to acknowledge how stupid it was to not bring either of my stakes. I got pretty good with those things this morning. There's no telling what I'm going to find inside.

Instead of turning back, I made a deal with myself. If the door is ajar, like it was before, I'm going keep walking and never look back. Any hint that those things are still around and I will be in the wind.

With that in mind I walk up to his door.

It's closed and locked.

I let out a relieved breath.

Before I break in, I decide to be sure. I make a slow tour of the perimeter of the house, checking the windows and the entrance to his basement. Around at the back door—which is also locked, by the way—I'm pleased to finally admit that the house is sealed up. Looking through the glass, I can even see the latch on the basement door. For the first time, the hook is through the eye. It has decided to stay latched.

Whispering apologies to Amber, I use a rock to break the glass and reach through the hole to unlock the door.

I'm already drenched in sweat. This day is turning out to be another miserable one. Mr. Engel's house is a good deal hotter. It's exactly what I would expect, and it's not a bad thing. As he told me—they hate heat.

Before entering fully, I close my eyes to see if I can sense any of the impending doom that I felt in their presence earlier. It's hard to say. My heart is already pounding from the act of breaking in, and I'm sweating from the heat. I think it feels okay though. Besides, I only have to go a few feet to reach the phone.

I take a breath and cross the room.

The line crackles with static, but I don't hear a dial tone.

I try to dial anyway.

Nothing happens.

"Hello?" I ask the static.

The sound of my own voice sends a chill down my spine and I can't take my eyes off the door to the basement.

That's it. I'm out.

I drop the phone and back out quickly, nearly slipping on the broken glass on the floor.

Once I'm outside, I catch my breath fast. Part of me wants to go back in and try the phone one more time, but I quickly overrule that idea. My gambling days are over. I would rather walk a few miles in the sun than go back in that house.

Back on the road, I turn around several times to glance at Mr. Engel's house. I'm sure that it was just nerves, but I'm still happy with my decision to leave. The only thing I'm not happy about is the garage. His keys were probably right in the kitchen, hanging on a hook. If Amber is going to forgive me for breaking in, she might have also forgiven me for borrowing the car.

It doesn't matter.

I'm perfectly capable of walking.

I pull the hat down to block the sun and I wipe sweat from my forehead. I jug of water would have been smart to bring.

It doesn't matter.

I have survived worse.

(I wish I had counted steps.)

I wish I had counted steps.

I wish I had brought a charging cord and tried to plug in my phone at Mr. Engel's, just to see if it would work.

I wish I had some water.

I wish I had grabbed a protein bar or *anything* from the pantry at home.

It doesn't matter.

I will survive.

One foot has to go in front of the other, regardless of what else happens.

I keep telling myself that I should be proud. I faced down the one with the violet eyes and I killed it in the name of Kimberly. Instead of giving in, I stood up to the allure of infinite bliss and I stabbed that creature to death.

But what if I'm wrong?

I don't have anything to prove the idea that those things were predators. Mr. Engel called them vampires in his delirious state. They tapped on a bunch of walls and windows and collected seeds on my porch. Are those reasons enough to warrant eradicating the whole swarm of them?

I keep thinking about the one in the freezer—the baby with the bluish violet eyes. That one was surely too young to have hunted anything. I killed the others because I suspected them of murdering Mr. Engel and because they were menacing me. I can't imagine that the baby did any of those things. I've never heard these things described. They're probably incredibly rare. I might have killed off the last pack of them. Their species may now be extinct because of my actions.

On either side of me, the tall grass is capped with tan clusters of seeds. There is precious little wind, but when it blows it sends mesmerizing ripples through the blanket of grass. I guess these are amber waves of grain? I never really thought about that before. It's like the Pledge of Allegiance. They taught us to memorize and recite that pledge, but it wasn't until much later that I really thought about what I was saying. I accept and endorse that pledge now, but at the time I started saying it, I didn't have the capacity to make such a deep promise. I don't believe they should have expected me to, either. It's like asking someone to sign a contract when they haven't learned how to read yet.

It's amazing how wet I am on the outside and how dry on the inside. Every time I try to swallow, my tongue feels like sandpaper on the roof of my mouth. Sweat keeps rolling down into my eyes so I can barely see.

I squint from beneath the brim of Uncle Walt's hat and keep my feet shuffling down the pavement.

There shouldn't be this much distance between the house and Prescott Road.

How is it taking this long?

There's a movie with Clint Eastwood called *The Good, the Bad and the Ugly* where Tuco makes Blondie march through the desert. Clint Eastwood looked like a piece of beef jerky by the end of that march. That's how I feel—dehydrated and sunburned. My lips are cracked and stuck together.

My wrist is throbbing.

I have been infected with something.

It's my last coherent thought.

The fall happens in slow motion, like the toppling of a monolith. My head leans too far forward and my feet are no longer able to keep up. I don't even get my hands in front of me. On the way down, my eyes go wide and the sunlight carves deep troughs in the back of my head. The amber waves of grain are tilting.

My limp body bounces on the gravel.

Everything goes light blue and then the light flares so bright that I can't see anything but white.

Sterile

(They don't know I'm awake.)

They don't know I'm awake.

Consciousness returns to me when I'm in the ambulance. At least that's where I assume that I am. My eyes are nearly closed, so everything is out of focus. I can see movement. That's about it.

I hear voices and I catch a word here and there. Most of it is just gibberish to me.

One of them is pushing up my sleeve.

I'm incapable of resistance. My senses work, but I can't seem to control my body.

If I could only get my eyes open, I'm sure I could communicate with them. They would see my stare and they would understand.

The world shifts beneath me and I come to know that we're moving. This is my world now. I'm trapped in this jostling, accelerating body, unable to make contact. It's somewhat like the pantry. At least they're not tapping.

Cool sanity flows back into me.

I'm able to blink.

The guy hovering over me looks familiar. Maybe we was

one of the guys who came for Mr. Engel?

He looks kind.

I was starting to worry that it wasn't an ambulance at all. I was starting to think that maybe I was inside of a refrigerator. Now that I can see his face, my panic subsides. I'm able to turn my head and I almost manage to get my mouth to form a word.

"Easy," he says, like he's trying to calm a rearing horse. "We'll get you there. Take it easy."

I think I'm strapped down because my arm meets resistance when I try to lift it.

"Easy."

When they roll me from the back of the ambulance, we pass through a shaft of sun. It burns my skin. At that moment, I make a wish—I never want to be in the sun's bright glare ever again. I'll do anything if that wish is granted.

They roll me into the air conditioned building and I nearly break into tears. It's so perfect in here.

I can relax for the first time in forever.

(The pain is a distant concern.)

The pain is a distant concern.

It must be the drugs. My body is alive with throbs and aches, but it doesn't bother me one bit. I'm perfectly content to stay perfectly still and listen to the sound of my own breath moving in and out of my lungs. The air is tranquil surf, rolling in and then disappearing into the sand.

My eyes shift, taking in the details of the room. The television is off. The lights in the ceiling are mostly extinguished. The blinds are halfway drawn. Through the gaps, I see clouds painted pink at the edges.

Everything is perfectly perfect.

Staring at the doorway, I see several people pass by before one glances over at me.

She stops in her tracks, regards me for a second, and then goes on her way.

I'm not surprised when she returns a few minutes later and asks me, "How are we feeling?"

It seems rude to answer for both of us, so I just smile at the question.

"Can you tell me what happened?"

I don't feel qualified to supply an answer to that. I give her another smile and I try to nod.

We go through this process for another few cycles before she gives up. I can't seem to communicate, but I'm not annoyed at all.

It must be the drugs.

It was wonderful when she was talking to me and it's still wonderful when she's gone.

I take a deep breath and let it out slowly. The air, in and out, becomes the crashing surf and it's lovely to listen to.

(I'm still in a fog.)

I'm still in a fog.

I've grown accustomed to the hospital schedule, but they've told me that it's time for me to go home. My body will recover more quickly if I don't spend too much time in a hospital bed.

"Aren't you excited to get back to normal life?" one person asks me.

I don't have an answer.

Honestly, I gave up on the idea of normal life a while ago. When I got to the point where I could form basic sentences, I started asking to talk with the police. They were eager to talk with me as well. I guess the state of my house left them with open questions.

An officer with a badge clipped to her belt came in and leaned very close to me to hear what I had to say. I told her about the knock on the door. I told her about my escape attempt, the fall, and then the truck. She blinked rapidly when I talked about the fuel line of the truck being cut and how I was forced to blow it up so I would have enough cover to get back to the pantry.

After that, I glossed over all the details until my walk back to humanity.

I included how I broke into Mr. Engel's house to try to use the phone. She nodded at that detail.

"Who do you think it was? Who tried to attack you at your house?"

"I don't have any idea. Did you find any evidence of them?"

Her eyes went up and around, bouncing from one corner of the room to the next until they landed back on me.

They all think I'm crazy.

That's the main reason I'm so surprised that they're so eager to send me home.

Once I've healed a bit more, they tell me that my regular doctor will help me make an appointment to be fitted with a prosthetic. For the staff in the hospital, my missing left hand is completely normal. They've only ever known me as the guy with the bandaged stump.

If I wasn't so drugged, I think that I would be appalled by the nub where my hand used to be. But, honestly, it seems perfectly normal to me as well. If anything, it seems like a temporary arrangement. When I get home, after some healing period, my hand will be right back where it belongs. I'm sure of that.

The first time I got up to use the bathroom, one of the nurses walked alongside me to make sure I wouldn't fall. I caught a glimpse of myself in the mirror and I shrieked. She jumped back, surprised for moment, and then her face went back to standard nurse's expression. They're usually unfazed by anything. If they register any emotion at all, it's annoyance. I'm not trying to paint a negative picture, I just think that part of their strategy is to treat everything with nonchalance. Perhaps that helps keep the patients calm.

I couldn't be calm at the sight of myself though. It wasn't just the missing hand. The color of my skin was completely wrong, and my eyes were horrifying. My eyes looked like they were nearly glowing with green fire. They were supposed to be brown. At least that's what I remember and that's what my driver's license says.

The nurse didn't care. She had found her way to nonchalance and she wasn't going to retreat from that stoic position.

Someone has laundered my clothes.

I button my pants with one hand using the plastic device they taught me to use. They taught me how to tie my shoes with only one hand as well, but I don't bother. I just tuck in the laces. They can't make me do it if I don't want to.

I check myself out and get into the cab they called for me. The driver takes me to get a rental car.

(The house looks the same.)

The house looks the same.

I know that the police have been here. The power company has removed the lines and put in a new pole, but they haven't hooked up the service yet. I'm supposed to just be here to pick up a few things and then go get a hotel room. That's what I told the officer.

They can't make me leave though.

I can stay here if I want to.

My wrist throbs as I walk into the kitchen.

There's bird shit on the floor. I sigh. I have to get cardboard, a utility knife, and some tape. For today, that will have to be good enough.

My uncle would have insisted that we fix the glass immediately. He was big on setting things right before he went to bed. Sometimes we stayed up until after midnight hanging a door or patching the siding. When I was a kid, staying up late felt like a precious treat.

At the moment, I just want to half-ass this repair enough so I can take a nap. Just being out in the daylight has tapped my strength.

In the hospital, when I first recovered the ability to communicate, I kept asking what happened to my hand. I guess I thought that if they couldn't give me a reasonable answer that they would have to give me my hand back. The different doctors all said the same thing.

"The infection was beyond treatment."

That's when I always asked the obvious follow up question, "What infection?"

Usually, the doctor would blink rapidly instead of answering. There was a lot of talk about biopsies and antibiotics. We were going to, "Watch and wait."

I guess that whatever they were watching for never came because I never heard much more about it.

Another part of me thinks that maybe the staff simply gave up. Maybe they decided that having me out of the hospital, away from the other patients, was a better strategy. At some point, when the fire is out of control, the fire department just stands back and makes sure that the flames don't spread to the neighbors.

With the windows plugged up with cardboard, I go out and sit on the stairs. The truck is gone—hauled away. There's still a scorched black section of ditch as a reminder. I don't last long on the stairs. Even though the sun is on the other side of the house, it's too bright out.

I go back inside.

Instead of heading through the living room and climbing the stairs to my room, I take a left. My picked jar of urine is still in the pantry. After I toss that in the dooryard, I close the door to the shed and push shut the door to the kitchen.

The darkness is almost perfect.

Part Five:

Rebirth

Growth

Night is better.

When I wake up, it's completely dark. My wrist both aches and itches, so I take off the bandage, intending to change it. It feels so much better when it's naked, that I just decide to leave it that way. The kitchen remains a disaster. I pull out the fridge as much as I can and I start to clean between it and the wall. In the beginning, I'm using tongs to move the larger items to the trash. By the end, I'm barehanding rotted food to the garbage can.

When I try to wash my hand, I remember that I don't have running water.

Everything seems helpless again. I want to go back to the pantry and hide from reality.

This time, I force myself to face my problems.

With my hand on the doorknob, looking out into the night, I realize something that should have struck me earlier—I don't have power.

I mean, I knew that before. They haven't strung up the new power lines. I have no power or water until they do, that's why the cops told me not to stay in the house.

I turn back to the refrigerator. The whole time I was

cleaning, it never once occurred to me that the lights weren't on. I didn't use a flashlight or anything, and it never bothered me. I suppose I was too distracted by trying to navigate the task with only one hand.

That's the only explanation I can come up with as I walk across the dooryard, around the barn, and head down to the path to the old well. The grass is tall. Despite the heat, everything grows fast in the summer in Maine. The plants know that they have a short window to establish themselves before winter.

I stop on the way and pick some berries. They're disappointing—crunchy and tasteless—until I find one juicy berry that makes it all worthwhile.

Uncle Walt maintained one summer well out near the pasture. It has a hand pump and the water that comes out is clear and sweet. I have to prime the pump with a scoop of disgusting water that has been sitting in the bucket, growing algae.

Once the water is flowing, I work the pump with my forearm and let the water spill over my dirty hand. I have to really take care of this hand now. It's the last one I have.

I laugh out loud at that and then I sigh.

I sit down in the grass and look up at the stars.

Will there ever be a time when things return to normal?

Am I ever going to get to a time when I can look back and make sense of this summer?

I got swept into an insane current and tried to ride it out. I suppose that I should feel lucky. With everything that happened to me, I just as easily could have died. Wasn't that the plan though? At some point, I think I decided that death would be better and I stalked death through that long night, trying to hunt it down. I offered it my throat and it wouldn't bite. All I lost was my hand.

When I spot another berry, I snatch it.

Halfway to my mouth, I inspect the thing. I want to make sure it's one of the good ones.

I blink at it for several seconds until I get a good look.

Scrambling backwards across the grass, I pitch the thing away from me. It wasn't a berry. It was a tick and I was about to put it in my mouth. The thought of that makes my stomach twist and lurch.

I push to my feet and head back towards the house.

If I had been thinking clearly, I would have brought a bucket or pitcher in order to take water back to the house. There will be plenty of time later, I suppose. I don't have anything else to do.

Rounding the corner of the barn, I see their lights coming down the road. We're on a collision course. The car that's coming to visit is going to reach my uncle's dooryard at the same time that I will. For a moment, I entertain the idea of running. I'm not expecting anyone, and I can't imagine that the visitor is bringing good news.

Then again, this is *my* house. I nearly died defending it. Why would I hide from company?

I straighten up and walk towards the kitchen door, raising my arm to shield my eyes from the headlights. When they get closer, I recognize the shape of the vehicle. It's the cops.

They stop just over the culvert. The driver turns off the engine and switches off the headlights. The house is still bathed in the amber glow of the parking lights.

I keep walking until I get to the side porch stairs. I stop and sit. I don't want to appear to be confrontational. In the hospital, I learned that cops are like caged dogs. They respond to aggression with aggression.

"Can I help you?"

I recognize her voice when she speaks. She's the one who first interviewed me after my amputation. She took advantage of my condition that time. I was still on really strong drugs.

"Didn't we talk about you getting a hotel room?" she asks.

"I will," I say. I've already slipped up. Why would I volunteer to do that? "I haven't finished cleaning up. It's going to be a long process."

"You need your rest," she says. "After what you've been

through, you need to take it easy for a while."

"Your concern is very kind," I say.

The person driving is leaning against the hood of the police car. The woman is still approaching.

I wish I knew my rights. Can I order them to vacate my property? I guess that would be a bad idea. The last thing I need is a combative relationship with the police.

"You're right on the line," she says.

"Pardon?"

I look down, wondering what line she's talking about.

"With a slightly different interpretation of the evidence out here, you could have been considered a suicide risk."

I narrow my eyes at her. She would be easy to take care of, I'm pretty sure of that. Her partner is too far away though. I shake my head, dismissing that weird thought. I've never been a violent person.

"Are you threatening to have me committed?"

"That's a hard thing to do," she says. "It's not so hard to hold you for a couple of days though. I actually argued to let you go on your way. In my opinion, you were still confused from heatstroke and infection. I thought that once you got back on your feet, you would be perfectly reasonable."

"Is there something unreasonable about wanting to clean up the house before I go find a hotel?"

She pauses, looking between me and the broken windows. I'm glad that I put up the cardboard. It gives her evidence that I've been working to fix up the house.

Her voice is softer when she speaks again.

"Please don't wear yourself out," she says. I can't tell if her kind tone is just an act. "I can see that you're tough, but don't underestimate what your body has been through."

I take a breath, count to three, and then let it out.

"Thank you," I say. "I'm just afraid that I would toss and turn all night with the house in disarray, you know?"

She smiles and nods.

"When do you get your power back?"

"Who knows. CMP is on their own schedule, as usual. They're probably charging me double for the electricity that I don't use."

That's something that Uncle Walt used to say. Mom would ask him why he didn't get a generator, and Uncle Walt would claim that Central Maine Power charges people double for every watt they *don't* provide.

She laughs. Nobody around here trusts CMP.

"You mind if we come and check in on you again in the future?" she asks.

I nod.

"Just yell if you don't see me. I could be out back or down in the cellar."

She is backing towards the car and waving.

She says something very quietly to her partner when she gets to the car. They're too far away from me for me to hear them, but I do anyway.

She says, "He's nuts, but I don't think he's dangerous."

They get in their car and drive away.

I watch until they're over the hill and then I listen to the engine until they're past Mr. Engel's house. I'm curious as to whether they will stop there and check on his empty house.

They don't.

(I have a visitor.)

I have a visitor.

The knocking wakes me and I sit up fast. There's a towel at the bottom of the door to block out the light. I move it aside and see that it's not too bright. The sun must be going down. I would have woken up pretty soon anyway.

I stand up in the pantry, smooth my hair with my hand and wipe my face. When I walk out of here, I want to look presentable, like I haven't been sleeping in the pantry all day.

It's probably the cops again.

When I open the door and emerge, I don't recognize the face on the other side of the kitchen door.

She spots me just as I'm deciding to slink back into the shadows of the pantry.

I wave with my nub and then slip it behind my back in embarrassment. In the hospital, one of the occupational therapists told me about proprioception. Maybe I'm remembering this wrong. He told me that I would likely still feel like I had a hand for quite some time. For a while, I shouldn't be surprised if I reach for things or try to wave with a hand that isn't there. It's still embarrassing.

The woman on the other side of the door doesn't seem to notice. She squints at me through the glass in the upper half of the door and I open it up, trying to smile.

"Hello?"

"Hi," she says. "I'm Amber."

For several seconds, the name doesn't help me at all. I simply stare at her with a dumb smile plastered on my face.

It comes back to me in a burst.

"Amber! Mr. Engel's... I guess I never knew your relation to Mr. Engel. You're too young to be his niece?"

She blushes and looks down. The rush of blood to her face makes her almost glow.

"Yes, grand niece, I guess. My mother was his youngest niece."

I nod and we stand there awkwardly for a moment.

"Sorry. Come in, I say."

I'm holding the door with my good hand so I gesture with my nub again.

"Oh, thank you," she says. She moves through the doorway carefully, like she's entering a cave and doesn't want to disturb any of the roosting bats.

When I turn and look at the kitchen through fresh eyes, I understand. The kitchen is dark and still smells of rotted food, despite my efforts to clean it up. There are large pieces of broken glass stacked on the counter. I'm not sure how to dispose of them without the shards poking through the trash bags.

"There was an accident," I say. I gesture towards a chair and take one for myself. "The truck exploded and broke the windows. It took down the power pole as well."

She nods. "I saw the power trucks today. Looks like they nearly have your house connected again."

I lean back to look through the window. She's right. The line is back up to the pole, and there's a brand new transformer installed there. Maybe tomorrow I'll have the electricity back. I'm not sure I still want it. The house seems just fine without it.

"I didn't think you were coming to town," I say.

"I figured I better check on the house," she says. "I had some time off and I realized that I hadn't seen the place in so long that I didn't even really remember what it was like, you know?"

I nod. I never had that problem with Uncle Walt's house. I knew this house better than any house my mother rented. Sometimes I would wake up in my bed in Virginia and expect to set my feet down on the wide floors of this house. It was always a shock to find out I wasn't at Uncle Walt's.

"Plus, I wanted to get a head start on figuring out what was in the house before my cousin gets there. Evan has sticky fingers," she says. She blushes again. "We're going to have a kind of lottery for everyone to pick the mementos that we want to keep. Everything else will get sold or donated, I suppose. Personally, I don't have any real attachment to his things, so I guess I will remove myself."

"That's kind," I say.

She starts to push back from the table.

"I didn't mean to come steal your time. I want to thank you for checking in on my uncle. I'm so glad that he didn't die alone, and that's because you were so thoughtful."

She looks at her hands and I can tell she's barely keeping in her emotions.

"It's okay," I say.

191

I reach out with my nub before I remember that there are no fingers there to comfort her with.

She glances and catches sight of it. I see her eyes go wide.

"The accident," I say. "I lost it in the accident."

It looks like a question has risen to her lips but she's too polite to ask it.

A silence grows between us. She opens her mouth to fill it.

"I don't know how you cope with the quiet out here. I was only in that house a few hours before I felt like I had lost touch with reality, you know? Maybe it's because my uncle's house is like a time capsule. Everything in the house is from 1960, it seems."

"Earlier than that," I say.

We laugh.

"And there's *nobody* around."

Her shoulders come together as a shiver passes through her.

"I used to come up a lot," I say. "Mom didn't know what to do with me in the summers anyway, so she sent me up to stay with my uncle. It's a slower pace, but you would be surprised. Even coming from the city, it doesn't take more than a day or two to settle into the rhythm. It's all about just looking around and seeing the world for how it is instead of what we expect it to be."

We fall silent again.

"Are you okay?" she asks.

I realize that my eyes are filling up. I wipe them away with my good hand.

"Can I..." she starts to say. A painful look crosses her face and then she puts it away. "I should go."

"No," I say. "You were going to ask me something, right? Ask it."

I feel really close to Amber. Maybe it's because we shared Mr. Engel. Maybe it's because we had almost completely different experiences with our uncles. Well, it was my uncle and her great uncle, but it's the same thing. Whatever the reason, I feel like Amber and I have a lot in common. I want her to ask whatever is on her mind.

"Please tell me to mind my own business if this is an impolite question," she says.

"Go ahead."

"You said you lost your hand in an accident."

"Yeah," I say. My nub is under the table, but it itches like it knows that it's the object of our conversation. "The same accident that burned up the truck and knocked out the power."

This is a slight exaggeration, but it simplifies the story.

"So... Is it..."

It's clearly terrifying for her to ask the question. Her curiosity compels her forward.

I raise my eyebrows.

"Is it growing back?"

I laugh. It feels good—all that happy air bursting from my chest. Of all the things I though she was going to ask me, this question never crossed my mind.

"No," I say when I catch my breath. "Of course not. It was so infected that they had to amputate it. Funny story—I never even got a clear picture on what the infection was. I mean, I know they had me on antibiotics through the IV. I'm still on pills now."

Actually, I had stopped taking the pills, despite the doctor's dire warnings to finish them.

"I'm so sorry for being nosey," she says.

"No problem," I say with a big smile. "I haven't gotten used to it, but I shouldn't be self-conscious, you know? It's just funny that..."

She cuts me off with, "I guess I saw a shadow or something. There isn't much light."

"No," I say. "Not until CMP gets their stuff together."

I don't mention that I have no intention of going back to electric light. After the last couple of days of communing with the darkness, I've come to enjoy it. Electric light would feel like a giant step backwards.

To set her mind at ease, I pull out my nub from under the table. I don't know if this happens to everyone, but I'm really embarrassed about my amputation. It's like some deep vulnerability that I desperately don't want the world to know about. I like Amber, and it feels like I can trust her, so I raise the nub over the table, into the last of the dying light in the kitchen.

The tentative smile disappears from her face as she leans forward a bit.

"I've taken enough of your time," she says abruptly. She's on her feet a moment later, making her way towards the door.

I guess it's going to be a long, long time before I let myself be vulnerable again.

"Thanks for coming by."

She's already showing herself out.

I watch her climb into her car. It's a rental. I bet she got it from the same place that I got mine. The headlights flare and I flinch back from the light, retreating deeper into my kitchen. Even her taillights appear impossibly bright as I watch her car disappear down the road.

That reminds me—I have to get rid of my rental car soon. It's probably costing me a fortune and I'm not using it at all. The details of the transaction seem impossible. How will I get back home?

I return to the table and slump into the chair. I just woke up a little while ago when Amber knocked. I'm still a little tired. I have the urge to go out and find more berries. Those perked me right up the last time I ate some. Nothing in the kitchen seems particularly edible. I might as well live off the land while it's providing. Winter is going to be a long stretch of hunger, I imagine.

Before I head out, there is one thing I need to really consider.

I reach back and pull open the third drawer down. My hand comes back with a stubby candle and then returns to the drawer for a box of matches. The occupational therapy class at the hospital never covered how to light a match one-handed.

Fortunately, I learned that trick when I was a teenager. I fold one of the matches over the end of the book and lay it on the rough strip. Then, aligning my middle finger and thumb like I'm going to snap, I strike the match. I snatch it up from the table before the whole book catches fire.

Even candlelight feels too bright to me.

If I'm being honest with myself, my eyes are the real problem with returning the rental car. The place is only open during the day. Even squinting through sunglasses, my eyes will never survive that long out in the sunshine.

I have to do one thing before I snuff the candle.

I have to really examine my nub and try to see it from the angle that frightened Amber. She was clearly driven away by what she saw. I know I took the bandage off way too early, I haven't been cleaning the area, and I stopped my antibiotics as soon as I left the hospital. The wound has every reason to be hideous and I've been ignoring it.

When I lift my nub into the candlelight, I understand Amber's horror.

The new flesh recoils from the light and tries to disguise itself amongst the sutures and puffy skin. I reach out with my good hand and pinch the flame between my fingers. Now that I've seen the shape lurking in the skin on my nub, I don't want to take my eyes off of it.

As soon as the candle is gone, the curious talons begin to emerge again. There are only two of them. The one near my ulna is the longer of the two. It looks like it has three full segments before it ends with a tiny claw. The other one—near my radius bone—is smaller. That one might only have two segments so far. I imagine that it's still growing. There's a bump on the side of the smaller one. Eventually, the bump is going to grow into a third boney finger, I just know it.

The long, alien fingers are searching around, tasting the air.

My heart is pounding as I try to figure out what to do.

I don't think I have the stomach to cut them off. Besides, why would I assume that removing them would help? They grew from the site of an amputation.

I lay my arm down on the table. The fingers retract for a moment and then reach out again. I know what they're going to do even before they do it.

As soon as they discover the flat surface of wood, the longer finger moves its claw perpendicular to the table and then taps.

TAP. TAP.

It pauses and both fingers turn a little, like they're listening.

My stomach twists and bunches.

These fingers don't belong to me. I wasn't even bitten by the thing upstairs—it just grabbed my wrist. But do I know that for sure? I didn't see what was happening under the bed. I assume that it reached out and grabbed me, but what if it was a bite?

The doctors told me about an infection that forced the amputation, but they were awfully cagey about the nature of the infection. I wonder what they saw.

TAP. TAP. TAP.

They listen again. They're taking stock of this room. They want me to eat. The idea seems to come from inside of me, but I'm sure that it really came from the fingers.

What kind of monster am I becoming? It's a ridiculous question. I know *precisely* what kind. I've seen them. I've killed them.

Amber eventually saw me for what I was. That's why she ran from the kitchen.

(I have an idea.)

I have an idea.

There's a distinct possibility that Amber would have been frightened away immediately, but she made the mistake of...

"Looking into my eyes."

I jump up and run for the bathroom.

I don't know how long it has been since I've used this bathroom. The medicine cabinet is set in the wall.

The last rays of sunset are almost extinguished. I wouldn't need them anyway.

I put myself in front of the mirror and then I look.

My eyes are twin galaxies, descending into infinity. They're not as luminescent as they will be. When they truly sparkle, Amber won't be able to look away, not after dark.

Even now, my eyes are almost so powerful that I'm entrancing myself.

"Mirror," I whisper. They used to say that vampires couldn't be seen in mirrors. Maybe the lore was twisted. Maybe the real message was that vampires couldn't look at *themselves* in mirrors. To gaze upon one's own infinite depths would bring paralysis.

I'm in danger of that now. It takes all my strength to push myself away from the mirror and flee the bathroom. I shut the door and vow to never go in there again. Fortunately, I've already banished the rest of the mirrors from the house. They're still down in the cellar.

The talons on my nub are waving around frantically.

They sense the thought that's still forming.

I have to put an end to this. I've already ruled out amputation. Even if it worked, the problem isn't just with my left arm. My eyes are infected as well. I should have guessed this already. It's not normal to be so sensitive to light.

The only answer is that I have to do to myself what I did to those other creatures. I have to find my stakes and then figure out a way to use them on myself.

Despair washes through me.

The idea of suicide is a betrayal of everything that has kept me going the last few years. I guess it should be a relief. After Mom died, I dragged myself back into the light. Kimberly kept me propped up until she was ripped from me. Uncle Walt was the last straw. He was the last real connection that I had to this world. I don't know why I'm still fighting.

That's not true.

I *do* know why I'm still fighting.

I'm fighting because Kimberly would have wanted me to.

She said, "Your darkness can't last forever. Light always wins."

Those words weren't meant to be a prediction. They were a prescription. She was telling me that I had to fight for life. I couldn't just let the tide overtake me and wash me out to sea. It's up to me to keep fighting.

What does that mean now?

How can I fight for life when I'm turning into the instrument of death?

"How do you know?" I whisper.

The voice seemed to come from outside of myself even though I felt the whisper on my lips.

"How do you know they were an instrument of death?" I ask myself.

I blink my giant eyes and move to the window.

The night is alive. My long claw taps on the glass and I see the ripples flow out as a yellow wave across the landscape. Anything moving appears as an orange flare while the sound of the tapping rolls out.

Sure, I'm a predator, but haven't humans always been predators? Haven't we always hunted, killed, and fed?

I push myself away from the window. These aren't my thoughts. These ideas are coming from the talons somehow. They're coming from my alien eyes. While I still have some control of my body, I have to do whatever I can to eliminate the idea that I might spread this curse to others.

Betrayal

(I'm afraid of not dying.)

I'm afraid of not dying.

Standing in the loft of the barn, I have a rope tied to the truss above. When I was a kid, my uncle wanted to replace the winch that was attached to this same truss. He stood up the ladder underneath and extended it all the way. It wasn't tall enough to reach the beam that spanned the main aisle of the barn. That beam was so high that barn swallows would nest up there and they wouldn't even stir while we moved below. They knew they were safe. While he was pondering how to get up there, I volunteered.

"I can use the step ladder to get to the beam from the loft and then shimmy across," I said.

He screwed up his face as he consider this idea. He started shaking his head, looking like he had just bit down on a lemon.

"You mother would kill me if she ever found out."

"I won't tell her," I said. I don't remember how old I was, but I was old enough to know that I wasn't supposed to keep secrets from Mom. She always said that there were no such things as secrets between adults and kids. If any adult asked me to keep a secret, I should nod and then run directly to her. She was smart that way. She stressed that it didn't matter who the adult was—friend, neighbor, principal, or relative. There were no such things as secrets between adults and kids.

But this secret was *my* idea. That meant that it didn't count.

Uncle Walt was still pondering the idea while I went and got the stepladder and carried it up to the loft. He was still shaking his head when I climbed up and straddled the beam. At that point, it was only an eight foot fall. As I worked my way around the first leg of the truss and out over the main aisle, the dirt floor of the barn was so far down that it made my head spin to even look. I kept my eyes straight forward and tried to ignore it. By the time I was out at place where the winch attached, I was terrified. All I had to do was reach under and remove the iron ring from the hook, but I couldn't do it.

When I finally admitted that to my uncle, he wasn't frustrated at all.

"That's okay," he said. "Just come on back. We'll figure another way. You know what? If I just pull the truck into the barn, maybe that will make the ladder tall enough."

Even before he finished, I knew that I wasn't going to be able to shimmy back to safety.

I broke out into a sweat and lowered my chest down to the beam, so I could wrap my arms around it. Without asking what I was doing, Uncle Walt figured out that I was having a panic attack. He shuffled off to go get the truck while I shivered and clung to the beam. For a little while after that, I was terrified of the idea of heights. I don't know if it's like this for other people, but I wasn't afraid of the idea of falling. I was afraid that I would lose control of my body. That's what happened up there. I kept telling myself that it was no big deal. If that same beam had been two feet off the ground, I could have done a thousand cartwheels on it and never stumbled. It was wide enough that I could have ridden a skateboard down the length. My body didn't listen to logic. As soon as I got out to the middle, everything shut down.

I couldn't even look as Uncle Walt arranged the truck and fetched the ladder. The extension ladder was so unwieldy that he usually had to wrestle with it for fifteen minutes to get it into position. That day, he was strong and confident. The legs of the ladder landed gently on the beam next to me and he climbed it in an instant. I trusted him completely when he guided my hand to the rung and then grabbed my belt loop and pulled me into position.

We moved down the ladder together, one step at a time. At the bottom, he told me to hold still while he dismounted. I sat on the gate of the goat stall and watched as he went back up and did my job for me. He and I never talked about the beam again. The next summer, I had my nerve back and I was able to help with the roof. Even with that, he didn't let me get too high on the roof before he called me back. He never mentioned the beam, but I suspect that it was in the back of his head. I was ashamed that I had failed him.

He would have been proud of me tonight.

Tonight, I jumped from the deck of the loft and grabbed the beam with my good hand. I was able to swing my legs up and then pull myself on top of the truss so I could walk calmly to the middle of the barn. I tied the rope a few feet away from where I had a panic attack when I was a kid. I'm fairly certain that I could have done a handstand on that spot and not wavered.

Once I got the rope into place, I walked back over to the edge and jumped back down to the loft. The occupational therapist never taught me how to tie a noose with one hand, but I figure it out. They should do that—teach amputees practical techniques for one-handed suicide. I bet it comes up fairly often.

Now, I'm standing here with the noose around my neck.

My talons snatch something from the darkness and stuff it into my mouth before I can react. Chewing it, I figure out that it has to be a spider. I have silky web stuck to my nub. I would spit it out, but it tastes really good. It's like eating a particularly tasty piece of scab, if that makes sense.

I can't live like this.

Maybe other people could cope with this alien transformation, but not me.

I step off the edge of the loft.

For the moment, everything is silent. I'll be flying for the rest of my life. It's nice to have everything planned out.

(I   e x p e c t e d   p a i n .)

I expected pain.

I'm gently swinging and the rope is creaking as I sway back and forth. My talons search for something solid to tap against. They want to send yellow waves out into the night to see what reflects back. I think I'm beginning to understand that compulsion. Tapping against solid objects with my claws is sort of like scratching a deep itch. The sound moves out into the world, but it also resonates through my own body. Now that I'm swinging in the air with nothing to tap on, my heart aches for that hollow sound.

After a few minutes of swinging, I realize that nothing is going to happen. I start to think about the others that I dispatched. One of them had only one eye. I can picture his suicide attempt fairly easily. Recognizing that he was changing over, I bet he tried to stab or shoot himself in the eye. Clearly, it didn't work. One of them had a stretched out neck. I wonder if that's what I'm going to look like when this is done.

I sigh and look around the barn.

I bet I could chew through the rope. It's just a stray thought, but when I run my tongue over my teeth, I start to believe it. They're not particularly sharp yet, but they will be. The flat bottoms of my front teeth are chipping away. My molars are splintering. If I just start chewing, my mouth with be full of razor-sharp daggers by the end of the process.

There's an easier way though. I kick off my shoes and brush one foot against the other. As I surmised, my toenails have already begun to sharpen. I reach up with my good hand, grab the rope above my neck, and then twist my body upside-down so

I can grip the rope with my feet. I can't even describe how it works, but it's the most natural thing in the world. After a couple of seconds, I'm back up on the beam, pulling the rope from around my neck. If I want to end this monstrous life, I'll have to find another way.

Once more, I'm thinking about that lonely train whistle. When I was a kid, I imagined a scene where the conductor stopped the train because he saw people on the tracks. Then, vampires overtook the train and drained the conductor of blood.

But what if the vampires were trying to commit suicide by stepping in front of the train? It's not a terrible idea. I shut my eyes and try to picture it. Even in my imagination, I can't do it. I can't hold still and let the train run me over. My body will react at the last second and I will jump out of the way, whether I want to or not.

It's starting to occur to me that I won't be able to do this alone.

I need myself from a week ago.

I need someone strong enough to take a stand against the abomination that I'm becoming.

Submission

(It seems like a good plan.)

It seems like a good plan.

I wait until it's almost dawn before I even think about moving into action. I had to tape the paper down to the table in order to write the note. Every time my left hand got close enough, it tried to scratch away the text or knock the pen out of my other hand. My only recourse was to sit down on my nub, as painful as that was, and write quickly.

I carry the note at arm's length just in case my talons want to try to shred it as I walk.

I don't take the road. There's never any traffic out here, but if there happened to be, I'm afraid of what the headlights would do to me. Even the stars seem really bright right now. My eyes aren't that good at recognizing shapes. For example, it took me forever to find a sheet of paper in my uncle's study. I had to consider the sheet of paper from several angles before I decided that it was what I was looking for. It was almost like I had forgotten the purpose of paper.

My eyes are sensitive as hell though. Far away from Mr. Engel's house, I can see the light that Amber left on upstairs. I have to circle the building so that I don't accidentally get a full look at the light as I approach. The back door is locked. She has already fixed the window that I broke when I tried to use the phone the other day. The windows are locked as well.

The best I can do is fold my note and wedge it in the gap between the front door and the frame.

My talons are itching on the inside.

I watch them reach out and I back away before they can tear up my note.

That wasn't what they were itching to do though. They're just as happy to reach out for the wood around the window. There are four distinct fingers emerging from my nub. There's a bump on the side that I think will grow into a thumb. The fingers are long and thin. They remind me of spider legs.

One claw rears back and then begins tapping.

The sound is so satisfying. Yellow waves roll out into the world and fill me with deep pleasure. Tapping is so enthralling and hypnotic. I can't imagine anything I would rather do.

When my second talon takes over for the first, the tapping is more insistent. It's building towards something. I try to track the imaginary yellow waves through the glass to understand their purpose. When I finally see it, I'm amazed and horrified. The sound of my finger hitting the wood is vibrating energy through the house and trying to focus it on the door lock. If they build enough, the vibrations will turn the mechanism and let me in. I imagine that it would take forever to move the deadbolt. There's so much mass there that I would have to stand out here for hours in order to turn that lock.

Something much smaller, like the hook on Mr. Engel's cellar door, that would go fast. That hook would slip from the eye in no time. If I were already in the cellar, I bet I could tap on the stairs and unhook that lock with so little sound that someone in the kitchen wouldn't even hear it.

It doesn't matter though. I won't be able to get inside. I've purposely left myself with very little time before dawn. The sky in the east is already beginning to warm up from black to dark blue.

I have to go.

I move fast across the fields. I only slow when my talons find something to eat. It's disgusting, but I know there's nothing I can do to stop myself from feeding. I'm too hungry to pass anything up. The talons only like things that consume blood. Ticks are their favorite. They'll also grab any spiders they can catch. At one point, I look down and see that I'm sucking on a furry corpse. I smack it away from my mouth with my good hand. There's no denying how good it tasted. Fresh from the animal, hot blood is incredibly satisfying.

I try not to think about it as I slip inside Uncle Walt's house and lock myself in the pantry. I'll need to find a safer place to stay eventually. The pantry is too exposed. I promise myself that I'll block up the cellar windows tomorrow night so that I can take refuge down there in the future.

At some point, it doesn't do any good to keep denying what I've become. I just have to make sure I don't lose sight of my real goal.

As I drift off to sleep, I try desperately to remember what it was.

(What was I thinking?)

What was I thinking?

I should have never come back to this pantry—it's too exposed. I swear I just heard a car engine. It wasn't a small engine, like the one that's in the rental car that Amber drives. It was the giant, throaty rumble of a serious engine. It was the type of engine that has horsepower to spare, crouched under the hood and ready to explode.

The sound has faded now. It's so low that I'm almost able to convince myself that it was a dream. Sometimes the sun finds a crack through the towel I have stuffed under the pantry door. Those stray sunbeams give me bad dreams.

The engine noise rises again and I understand what's happening. The vehicle passed behind the hill between Uncle Walt's and Mr. Engel's. It's getting closer. I recognize it now. It's the sound of the police car.

I hear gravel crunch as it rolls across the culvert.

The driveway chime rings. Those crooks from CMP must have reconnected the power. So maybe it wasn't the sunlight that gave me bad dreams. Maybe it was the sound of the workers that infiltrated my daytime slumber.

It's her—the policewoman. I hear her footsteps in the dooryard followed by another pair. Her partner is moving very cautiously. I can hear it by the way he puts his toe down first and then rolls his weight to his heel. They suspect that I'm dangerous.

KNOCK. KNOCK. KNOCK.

She calls my name.

I'm paralyzed. I couldn't answer if I wanted to.

KNOCK. KNOCK.

She calls again.

I hear her partner whisper to her, "Open door over here."

He must be talking about David's door. I think I might have left it ajar. My heart starts pumping, sending energy up to my eyes. I'm going to need them. David's door creaks on its hinges as the partner pushes it open. I hear him settling his weight on the shed floor. His uniform rustles as he peers around the corner, looking for me.

He has to go away, right? They can't just come into someone's...

He takes a step and I hear her climb up onto the stone apron under David's door.

They're coming in.

He makes a brief detour down to the barn while she waits. They whisper back and forth in quick bursts.

"Shop. Wood pile," he says.

"Any blood? Tracks?"

"Nope."

I hear a click and then very low crinkling hum. He turned on the shed lights. Again, what was I thinking? I could have turned off the breakers for the whole house before I went into the pantry. I should have known that CMP would be by eventually. This was simply a lack of foresight.

"Noose," the partner says.

He makes a quick survey of the first floor of the barn and then his feet come back through the shed to stop at David's door.

They consult in low voices.

"Maybe he dropped off the note and came back here to kill himself," the partner offers.

"But didn't do it?" she asks.

"Not by hanging," he says. "Keep going?"

"Let's see if the door to the house is open," she says.

That's my door—the pantry door—that she's referring to. I still can't move. I can barely open my eyes. They're both creeping. They're coming down the shed hall towards my position and there's nothing I can do about it. My eyes are throbbing in the darkness. This must be how the mother felt when I was descending into Mr. Engel's basement. She was waiting inside the chest freezer, hoping that I would go away.

They stop at the door. I hear one of them nod their head. A hand touches the doorknob.

"Locked," she whispers.

"Now what?"

She sighs.

"This is my fault. I knew I should have pushed harder to get him under observation. He's probably on the bathroom floor with a stomach full of pills," she says.

"Why write a note asking the neighbor to kill you and then come home and do it yourself?" he asks.

I hear the policewoman shrug.

So this is about the note that I left for Amber. She must have called the police as soon as she found it. I trusted her and she snitched on me and my plan to end my life. They're going to keep looking for me. This policewoman feels guilty about failing me and I bet she is going to keep trying to track me down. Maybe they're going to go get a warrant and come back to search the house. '

That idea enrages me. This was Uncle Walt's house. How dare they try to come in here without permission?

If I could only move, I could fix this problem right now.

I've developed this problem though. When the sun is above the horizon, even if I can't see it, I have a problem moving. I think that if I were stronger I might be able to move. I've been living on meager rations of ticks and spiders. That's not enough to sustain me.

I have to try.

With all my effort, I manage to tap one of my talons against the floor.

On the other side of the door, the woman catches her breath to listen. The man opens his mouth to say something and I hear her shirt move. She must be gesturing for him to be quiet.

I tap again.

The doorknob rattles and my talon gains a little strength. Energy pulses through me as the imaginary yellow waves flow out from my percussive sound. My tapping picks up a rhythm and I focus my concentration on the door lock. This mechanism is much smaller and lighter than the deadbolt at Mr. Engel's house. With just the right series of taps...

The lock clicks.

I stop tapping.

I know the policewoman heard it. I can sense her focus. Her muscles are tensed. She must be staring at the knob.

"What was that?" the man asks.

"I don't know. I think the door is unlocked though."

"Should we try it?"

"I don't think so," she says. Her instincts are serving her well. That's bad news for me.

(I don't know why she changes her mind.)

209

I don't know why she changes her mind.

All I know is that I hear the knob as she grips it. I hear her fingers clench and my beating heart sends all of my energy to my eyes. When the door opens and the sliver of electric light begins to invade my space, I'm ready for her. The light touches my toes and she peers around the edge of the door. I catch her in my stare.

I absorb her conscious mind into mine. It's as easy as catching a bird that's fluttering against the inside of a window pane. I fold my thoughts around hers and capture her will. She is completely hypnotized by my stare.

It only takes a moment for her partner to realize that she's frozen. He kicks the door open the rest of the way as he takes a step back. The shed lights wash over my skin. It's terrifying to feel the rays of light penetrate me. Little explosions of pain erupt all over as I try to hold the woman's eyes and capture the man's at the same time. My heart is pounding inside my chest at the exertion. I wrap both of their minds together inside mine and bind them in the swirling spirals of my eyes. They fight me. These people are strong.

There's no way for me to hold them as I burn in the electric light.

The man's hand is right near the switch.

I push on his mind, trying to exert myself. At first, all he does is twitch and sway. This is like trying to operate a remote control car while it's heading directly towards me. I have to reverse everything I see in order to manipulate his left hand. Finally, I get him to raise his hand and flop it towards the switch. When his fingers smash against the switch, the shed lights go out and relief floods through me.

In that moment, I lose the woman.

She manages to look away, breaking my hold on her.

She reaches for her gun.

This is what I've been hoping for, isn't it? I wanted

someone to put me out of my misery before I could transform into a monster. I've already changed much more than I would like to admit. All she has to do is point that deadly piece of metal and pull her trigger and this will be over. Hanging didn't work, but I'm sure that scrambling my brains with a bullet will do the trick.

It's not up to me though.

The infection has engendered lizard instincts inside me that I can't control. Just like I forced him to turn off the lights, my hypnosis forces her partner to fall on her, knocking the muzzle of her gun away from me at the same moment that she pulls the trigger.

The blast appears wonderfully beautiful at first. I see the waves of pressure come from the muzzle as they escape with the projectile. They're bright orange and yellow, like the sun on a perfect day. Bouncing off the walls and officers, the ridges of sound light up everything in perfect detail. Then, in an instant, the first sounds begin to hit my ears.

The assault rings like chaos inside my skull. I shrink back, shrieking in pain as the bullet plows into the wall and the sound echoes inside the pantry. The gunshot drives hot spikes into my eardrums. I lose my control over the man.

They both flinch back at the sound of the gun.

I'm already recovering. The sound was horrible, but my body bounces back fast.

I focus on her as she raises the gun in slow motion.

I'm staring into her eyes and I can also see right down the barrel of the gun. Her fingers are squeezing, trying to pull the trigger again. Just before the hammer is tripped, my mind slips around hers. I wrap her up in a heavy blanket of hypnosis.

The man falls into my trap as well.

She lowers her gun and I let out a relieved breath.

I still can't move anything more than my talon. For the moment, it's all I need.

While I hold them in my stare, I tap on the floor. I let the echoes ring out until I'm sure that I'm hearing them correctly again. The sound soothes and comforts me, but it also does more. I think the sound is actually helping me heal from the sound of the gunshot. It also helps to mesmerize the police officers. I'm able to blink my enormous eyes without losing my grip on them.

I send the yellow waves down into the cellar below me and direct them to show me the details of the breaker box. It takes a while, but I build up enough energy to trip the main breaker for the house. The hum goes away and the threat of electric light is gone for good.

Meanwhile, the officers are enthralled with my eyes.

The sun is still descending on the west side of the house and I'm gaining strength as it does.

It's really lucky that Amber didn't call the police earlier. She must have missed the note that I tucked into the door.

I feel the minds of the officers squirm inside my control.

I'm able to hear them inside my head. I have a sort of telepathy with them.

"You shouldn't have come," I tell them.

The policewoman is able to form a response that I understand. "You asked us to."

"No," I tell her.

Is she right? What did I say in that note? I asked for Amber's help. It was because I didn't trust the police to do the right thing. I thought that they would shrink from the responsibility of ending my life. I wanted a guarantee that they wouldn't try to put me in a jail cell. If they managed to confine me, it would just be torture. I wanted my life to be over.

So why did I just stop her from shooting me?

I could do it now.

I used the man as a puppet. The gun is still in her hand.

In fact, why not both?

I massage the man's mind until his hand reaches, draws his gun, and clicks off the safety.

It's easy to get them to do things that they already want to do. They're both exerting pressure back on me now. They want to squeeze their triggers, sending bullets ripping through the infinite space inside my eyes.

"Do it," I whisper.

The woman's hand trembles in time with her lower lip. There's a battle inside her that I'm not privy to. The man's hand begins to tremble as well.

They either can't or won't do it. It should be easy enough for me to force their fingers to squeeze the triggers, but now there's a battle inside of me as well. The part of me that links my mind to theirs has a decent amount of self-preservation. I can't manipulate them into killing me.

(I'm stronger than ever.)

I'm stronger than ever.

The man was easier. I nudged and pulled at his mind until he was leaning forward. His arms slumped to his sides. The gun was forgotten completely. When he was within reach, my talons guided him forward and opened him. It's not like consuming food. It's the absorption of energy. The effect is instantaneous. There is no waste involved.

I understand why spiders are so delicious.

They consume and concentrate energy. Think of how much energy a fly has. They can buzz around constantly for days. The spider pulls that power right from the center of those insects and leaves behind everything else. A tick latches onto a host and sucks energy in the same way.

I'm the ultimate parasite.

I take the man's energy, or spirit, or soul—whatever you want to call it—and I incorporate it into myself. I could have left him with enough power for his body to eventually recover, but I don't. I take his energy down to zero. As I taste the last of it, I feel him inside me and I know that my transformation is complete.

There's nothing human left inside of me now except a tiny scrap of decency.

Urging the woman to come forward, I vow to leave her with a beating heart.

She was trying to protect me from myself.

I guess they both were, but he's already dead.

I'm still pondering this irrational favoritism as she draws her final breath. Their bodies litter the doorway for the moment. They're already beginning to decompose into unstable slime. In a few minutes, before I've even finished collecting myself, the only things left are clothes, tools, and weapons. My talons push these remnants around. I look at my other hand—my good hand. These eyes aren't so adept at specific details of things. It's much easier to understand the world around me when I can tap.

I use the new talons on my good hand to tap on the wall. I see yellow waves bouncing and all the shapes perfectly outlined. My body has transformed. Clothes are hanging off of me. I don't need them. I gather up the police clothing. One of them had a pocketful of change that has spilled. I have to pick up each coin so I can sort them into proper piles. This isn't a thing that I *want* to do—it's necessary.

Outside, night has fallen. I skirt around the cone of light from the vehicle and shut everything off. I take the keys and add it to the stack I've made in the dooryard. Shoes, socks, pants, undergarments, shirts, gadgets, weapons, and keys are all sorted and stacked. I can't close the door on the vehicle until I pick up all the poppy seeds that someone has littered on the upholstery. My talons do the work while I listen to the night.

Amber is still out there.

She will fix all this for me.

First, just to make everything neat and tidy, I take all the police gear out to the old well. I let it all drop in the water and listen to it as it sinks below the surface.

I'm not describing this right. My brain still thinks that it's in control. In reality, I'm watching all of these things happen with my imperfect eyes. All these tasks are pure instinct. My legs move me around. My hands have their own plans. My nose keeps turning to the wind to add to our knowledge of the world. I'm no more in control than someone watching a movie. Sometimes what's happening on the screen makes perfect sense. Other times, like when I stop to count the stars, I have no idea why I'm doing the things that I'm doing.

I'm a passenger.

(The light doesn't bother me.)

The light doesn't bother me.

I'm much stronger now. Amber has every light on the first floor of Mr. Engel's house on. It's a hot night, but all the lower windows are closed. From a distance, my eyes watch her shape move through a rectangle of light. She's looking in the direction of my uncle's house. I bet she's watching for the return of the police. They've been gone a while now.

I see her moving to the kitchen and I remember the phone on the wall.

I'm not conscious of any intention that I have to stop her from contacting the outside world. My arms and legs propel me through the grass anyway. Soon, I'm at the front corner of the house where the phone line emerges through the foundation and connects to the phone box. One of my talons pushes through he insulation and interrupts the connection. It was a new wire. They must have replaced it recently. They're going to have to replace it again.

I hear her inside the house, practically shouting at the phone.

I know the feeling.

We've grown so accustomed to being in constant contact with the world. A small amount of isolation is terrifying.

When I was a kid, I resented my mom's phone calls when I visited Uncle Walt. She always wanted to know details about what projects we were working on and what I had learned. Those intrusions sucked the life out of the lessons that I learned. When I had to encapsulate my accomplishments into words, their size and importance shrank. I eventually resorted to monosyllabic responses to her questions. She got the point eventually and called less frequently.

While my brain recalled that memory, my body was busy.

I'm clinging to the side of the house, lifting the sash of one of the bedroom windows.

I try to yell to Amber to tell her to run. She has to run before my eyes snare her.

I pause at the top of the stairs and tap on the bannister. It's not to find her—I already know that she's in the kitchen. I can hear her rapid breathing. When I really focus, I can hear her pounding heart. I'm tapping because it's an innocuous sound. It will draw her closer to me.

I'm also tapping to find the switch at the bottom of the stairs. If I can get it to flip, the lights in the downstairs hall will be extinguished and I can move closer to her. We'll meet in the middle and she'll get to see my eyes. I think she will like them.

The switch is easy enough to locate, but it won't flip. It should be well within my power, but it won't flip. Everything in Mr. Engel's house is old. It's probably rusty.

Everything in Mr. Engel's house is old.

That means that the lightbulbs are probably old too. They probably have those old, delicate filaments that could easy be vibrated until they break. As soon as my talons receive that information, they shift their focus to try to shake the bulbs. My eyes inform them that their efforts aren't working. The yellow waves come back from the bulbs. They're not moving like they're glass and filament. The bulbs have been replaced with newer types. These aren't fragile lightbulbs at all. Amber must have wanted to save money on the power bill.

I think about the breakers in the basement. I managed to flip one in my house. I can probably do the same thing here.

Just as I start to tap, music blares down in the living room below. It's loud and the bass thumps. There's nothing I can do against this onslaught of vibration. It effectively cancels any tapping that I might do. I've lost one of my primary senses and one of my strongest powers.

It will be uncomfortable, but I think that my body will be able to handle the lights downstairs. All I have to do is get close enough for Amber to look into my eyes and then I can get her to shut off the lights for me. Actually, it would be best if she shut off the music first. That sound is horrible.

It's...

"The Mountain of Pure Rock," the voice says. After a thunderclap and a gong, AC/DC plays.

Amber didn't strike me as a WTOS fan. I guess I misjudged her.

If it were up to me, this would be a good time to leave. The bedroom window is still open. Climbing up was simple. I'm sure that getting back down will be even easier. I'm still full of power and I don't have a particular hunger for Amber.

The problem is the letter and the snitching. She called the police once and she has paper evidence to back up her claim. I don't remember what I wrote, but it was enough to get the officers to my house. They're probably going to keep looking for me. Maybe if I get rid of Amber and the letter, I'll find some peace.

My legs have already decided on this course of action. I'm slipping down the stairs, trying to hear Amber over the screeching AC/DC.

The music makes it difficult to think.

I creep down the stairs, slowly exposing myself to the light down there. The glare is painful—as bad as the music, really—but I think I can tolerate it long enough to find her.

I'm almost to the bottom of the stairs and I'm clinging to the left wall. That's where the deepest shadows are. I think I understand why the light is so horrible. My skin is working hard to try to make me blend into the shadows. That's not something I can control. It's as automatic as blinking, which I don't seem to do as much anymore. I would say that it's as automatic as my heart beating, but I don't think my heart still beats during daylight.

Anyway, my skin is good at disguising me, but direct light is way too much work. When one of my talons strays into the light, my arm snatches it back. It needs time to recover.

Complete darkness would be the best way to recover. On the other side of the bannister, there's a hall closet. The door is ajar. It would be an ideal refuge.

Bracing myself for the light, I spring up, leap over the banister, land softy on the floor and then slip into the closet.

Relief floods through me. The coats muffle the sound and the door blocks out the light. After a few minutes in this solitude, I'll be ready for anything. I slip to the very back and huddle down with the overshoes and a stray set of gloves that must have fallen from the shelf. It smells like Mr. Engel in here—like a towel, fresh from the dryer.

I won't, of course, but I could stay here forever.

In the living room, the Mountain has finished with AC/DC for the moment and I hear a commercial for some car dealership. Are they the only advertisers? It seems like the only business I hear ads for.

The radio clicks off and I can't believe my luck.

My talons don't waste a single second.

They tap on the floor, echo into the basement, find the breaker and switch it off. The light under the bottom of the door goes out. I hear Amber take in a sharp breath—she's right outside the closet door—and then I hear something that almost sounds like rain.

A grain of rice bounces under the door and lands on the toe of a boot.

My talon shoots out and snatches it up.

Her heart is beating fast and she's practically gulping down air. She's not trying to run. I can sense her, on the other side of the door and a few feet down the hall.

All I have to do is open the door wide enough and she will

see my eyes. That's all it will take.

I shift silently in the dark. A ripple travels through my skin so it won't rub against the coats and make them move. A talon puts a tiny amount of pressure on the door, making it swing open slower than a minute hand.

Amber is still standing there. I don't know what she's doing, but it won't matter soon.

If I were her, I would already be running. Three paces between each breath would keep my stamina as I fled out into the night, but Amber is just standing there.

Even in the dark, I can see the grains of rice. The rice hitting the floor was what I thought sounded like rain. She must have spilled the dry rice when the lights went out and now she's frozen in fear.

It won't matter soon.

I push the door open a little wider so I can pick up the rice. My talons need to do that before my eyes will be free to mesmerize Amber.

"Hey," she says.

Even with her heart racing and her breath coming in quick gasps, she sounds calm. I guess I misjudged her adrenaline for fear.

The flashlight clicks on and I see the beam coming towards me.

It that last moment, I lock eyes with her.

I sense her mind and I hear my own words echoing in there.

They're from the letter.

"If I don't knock on the door, like a friendly neighbor, then please understand that I'm here to do you harm."

Another tidbit floats by just before the light hits me.

"You'll know I'm close if you hear tapping. Scatter seeds to slow me down."

I must have given her more advice than that. I see that the flashlight is taped to a long wooden stick. She's gripping it in both hands.

Amber drives it forward into my right eye.

I remember the whole letter.

I thought she would be unable to resist my stare. I'm so strong now from the two police officers. Amber jerks her stake back with a grunt and shoves it into my other eye.

I can still see the yellow waves. They're a part of everything that moves or vibrates. The echoes of her heartbeat light up the hallway and the rice on the floor. They show me everything even as the world begins to melt.

Then, with a long exhale, the world turns to mist and disappears.

(Letter)

Dear Amber,

You don't know me well, but I shared a moment with Mr. Engel. I hope you'll remember that as you read what I have to say. Give me the benefit of the doubt even though what I'm writing is going to sound crazy.

I'm going to try to come to you tomorrow, after dark. I can't come until the sun goes down. I'm going to ask for your help. The infection that killed your great uncle is attacking me. It's turning me into a monster, and I can't live this way. You saw the talons growing from my wrist. The change has progressed since then. If I could take my own life, I would. I've tried. I need your help to end this.

I know that this is a lot to ask.

Hopefully, I will still be able to explain this in person when I come to you. If I can't, then that means the infection has already gone too far. If I don't knock on the door, like a friendly neighbor, then please understand that I'm here to do you harm. You'll know I'm close if you hear tapping. Scatter seeds to slow me down.

My eyes are hypnotic. Even glancing at them can cause

paralysis. That's how the infection traps its next victim. Light is the antidote. A flashlight can diminish the mesmerizing effect. I killed thirteen infected, most with a wooden stake—not through the heart, but through the eyes.

Sharpen something wooden to a point. I used a shovel handle and a broomstick. It's not hard to pierce the eyes. Trust me, you'll know it's necessary when you see what I have become. We move in the darkness or shadows, hunt at night, and use our claws to tap so we can listen to the echoes. We hide during the day. Any scratch or bite can transmit the infection. Don't let me get too close.

I hope you can read this. It has been a battle to write this letter.

Sincerely,

Ike Hamill
September 2019
Topsham, Maine

About *Until the Sun Goes Down*

This book was a lot of fun for me to write. I hope you had as much fun as I did. Books with monsters—real or imaginary—have always been my favorite. I take that back. I'm actually not too fond of the imaginary sort of monsters. A scary book needs to have a payoff. There has to be something unexplainable or else I'm a little disappointed.

With *Until the Sun Goes Down,* our narrator is driven more by his own fear than anything else. Did those creatures really mean him harm? Do we have any irrefutable evidence? In a lot of horror stories, the characters are doomed because they refuse to act while they try to explain everything away. In this story, I wanted the narrator to jump to a quick conclusion and act accordingly. It was just rotten luck that he still got tripped up.

When I was a kid, I used to come to Maine every summer to stay with my grandparents at their house in the middle of nowhere. The house was on a dirt road. At night, the light on the barn made a tiny patch of safety surrounded by endless woods that contained countless horrible monsters. That place terrified me and I loved it.

'Salem's Lot came out in 1975. I don't remember what year I found a dog-eared copy, but I know exactly where I was when I read it. I had come up that year without my brother and sister, and I was staying alone in the guest room with the twin beds. It was a scorcher of a day, filled with swimming and chores in equal measure. That night, with the window open, a breeze finally brought relief from the heat. I got up and closed it anyway, because I was reading about *'Salem's Lot,* where the dead can't seem to stay still.

I even pulled the shade, afraid that I would see glowing eyes hovering outside the second-story window. That book made me afraid to even take in a deep breath. I hope that one of my books gives that kind of thrill to someone. I treasure that memory.

Hope you liked the story. If you haven't read my other books, you should check them out. I have a bunch. *Stay Away* and *Fiero's Pizza* are in a similar vein. *Migrators* takes place a few miles from this book and shares some of the same atmosphere. Let me know what you think. You can find me on Facebook, Twitter, or email (ike@ikehamill.com).

All my best,
Ike

Stay Away

Every small town has secrets. Some secrets can kill.
He's always been there, the old gentleman in the funeral suit,
hanging around the big oak tree. Even before the cemetery was
dug, the natives knew about him. He was just as much a part of
the landscape as the rocks or the river. If you ever needed
anything, especially if it was a matter of life and death, you could
find him and make a trade.

He always trades fair. Everybody says so.
Eric is about to trade without even realizing it. He isn't tricked.
It's only a mistake. "Caveat emptor," some might say. Uncle
Reynold would say, "Watch your butt, lest somebody kicks a new
hole in it."

Fiero's Pizza

There's something out there waiting for your family and it needs you to call. Your baby can sense it. In the middle of the night, when the curtains blow, you can sense it too. All it needs is an opening. Once it's inside you, it will control everything.

What if your family is already doomed?

Brian and Samantha have found the perfect home to start their family. It's an old farmhouse in rural Maine, with plenty of character and plenty of room to grow. And they're just in time! Before they've moved in, Samantha goes into labor with their first son. With the house, they get more than they bargained for. They stumble into the clutches of a demonic parasite, just waiting to latch onto the next family. By the time they realize what is happening, their fate is already sealed. Only their love and commitment to each other will see them through. But what if they're not strong enough?

Time to call Fiero's Pizza -- FREE Delivery -- Now Open Sundays!

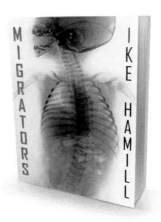

Migrators

Do not speak of them. Your words leave a scent. They will come. Somewhere in the middle of Maine, one of the world's darkest secrets has been called to the surface. Alan and Liz just wanted a better life for themselves and their son. They decided to move to the country to rescue the home of Liz's grandfather, so it would stay in the family. Now, they find themselves directly in the path of a dangerous ritual. No one can help them. Nothing can stop the danger they face. To save themselves and their home, they have to learn the secrets of the MIGRATORS.

Made in United States
North Haven, CT
11 June 2023

37611470R00138